THE DEFENDER
A NOVEL
ILLUSTRATED
BOOK ONE

By
Harvey Tingle

DEDICATION

This book is dedicated to my wife, Charlotte, who gave me two sons and the best life any man would want.

CONTENTS

One: An Unhealable Wound 1

Two: A Strange Encounter 5

Three: Can this be Real? 7

Four: Adventure Ahead 10

Five: Who is Ryan Logan? 13

Six: Eavesdropping in a Tavern 15

Seven: Skipping a Week 17

Eight: A Cowboy Needs a Horse 20

Nine: Into Another World 22

Ten: Down an Old Wagon Road 24

Eleven: Country Life on the Frontier 26

Twelve: Home in Appalachia 33

Thirteen: Where Has Our Protector Gone? 34

Fourteen: Gramy and Grubby 36

Fifteen: Insulting a Frenchman 37

Sixteen: Slowly Flying Arrow 39

Seventeen: For All 41

Eighteen: Blow Up 42

Nineteen: No Big Deal, Only a Forest Fire 44

Twenty: A Perplexing Problem 46

Twenty-One: Hundred Year Jump 48

Twenty-Two: Is That Preaching? 51

Twenty-Three: Praying, Parties And A Whooperup 52

Twenty-Four: Tom Mitchell Family 57

Twenty-Five: Great Cornbread 58

Twenty-Six: Katy, Katy 60

Twenty-Seven: In the Jailhouse Now 62

Twenty-Eight: Insult to Injury 64

Twenty-Nine: Confronting a Banker 65

Thirty: Jailbreak Anyone? 67

Thirty-One: Posse Anyone? 69

Thirty-Two: Wind-Blown Grime to the Rescue 70

Thirty-Three: St Louis, Really? 71

Thirty-Four: Riverboat Disaster 73

Thirty-Five: Old Friend, New Friend 76

Thirty-Six: Rescue Turns to Murder 77

Thirty-Seven: You're the Pastor? 79

Thirty-Eight: Looking over the Town 83

Thirty-Nine: Scrumptious 85

Forty: Worship Interrupted 88

Forty-One: Looking Ahead 91

Forty-Two: Con Man 92

Forty-Three: Fearful River Crossing 94

Forty-Four: Repulsive Reception 97

Forty-Five: Dealing with Disappointment 99

Forty-Six: A Bully Gets His 101

Forty-Seven: A Railroad Even 104

Forty-Eight: Storm's on the Way 106

Forty-Nine: Traveling Far From Home 109

Fifty: Is This The End? 111

Fifty-One: Can This Be Lubbock? 114

Fifty-Two: Bank Robbery in the Making 117

Fifty-Three: Dumb Doras 119

Fifty-Four: Propitious Retreat 120

Fifty-Five: Overcoming a Dropout 122

Fifty-Six: Tutoring in the Extreme 124

Fifty-Seven: On a Steak Out 126

Fifty-Eight: Attitude Adjustment 129

Fifty-Nine: Visiting an Old Friend 131

Sixty: A New Dilemma 133

Sixty-One: Bring $5,000 137

Sixty-Two: A Never Ending Search 140

Sixty-Three: Is This Mother? 144

Sixty-Four: Methamphetamine Or Crank 147

Sixty-Five: Back to Belinda 151

Meet The Author 154

ILLUSTRATIONS

Bob Becker, High School Teacher 3

Malek, Special Agent 8

Belinda, Bob's Fiancé 12

Appalachian Home of Ryan and Teata 29

Teata 32

Charlesville .69 Caliber, French Musket 38

Coon Creek Camp Meeting 56

The Glenco Explodes 74

Louis Remey 82

Sheriff Bruce Barton 103

Dr. Steve Bancroft 136

Mrs. Jamila Wilson 142

ONE:
AN UNHEALABLE WOUND

Lifting his hand from the steering wheel, Bob looks at his watch. He runs the same thought through his mind for something like the tenth time: *Why does this happen to me?*

He slaps the steering wheel. Struggling to avoid thinking about it, still, those words haunt him. "I'm afraid I have some bad news for you, Mister Becker."

The image of Dr. Paul Langly tromps through his mind. He's heavy-set with a receding hairline. *That brown hair is blended with silver. Under a bulbous nose, lives a straggly mustache.* Recalling how repeatedly he pointed his finger at him, he flirts with the idea, *That man's more than a little condescending. Next time I see him, I'm gonna tell him, to stop pointing that finger at me.*

Half an hour later, he's sitting on a park bench. Dozens of thoughts are contending to be heard. His mind churns as his stomach tightens. *Feel like I'm drowning, like I'm falling down a deep, dark hole. Maybe I should see another doctor. How do I tell my fiancé?*

How did I get this? When do I tell my employer? What do I do about all the plans I had for my life? How long do I have? Plainly, he has a divided mind with all sides struggling with the others.

Once again, unbidden, Dr. Langly intrudes in his head. *He has a low, rough voice, like a sore throat*, Bob says, w*ith a serious face. I can't bear to repeat what he said.* Without invitation, tears begin trickling down both cheeks. Barely above a whisper, he mumbles, "I always wanted to make a difference." Then again, for the thirtieth time, he utters, "Why?"

The open wound in his heart won't heal. His trembling lips are reflections of the shaking inside him and salts in his mouth are from bitter tears.

Suddenly, something catches his eye. *Is it real? Am I imagining it?* Whatever it is, it's vaporous and airy. It's also semitransparent. Beyond that, it's also somehow alluring in a mysterious, haunting way. *It's mystifying.*

In a matter of seconds, it solidifies into the form of a man.

"Unbelievable!" He's tall, over six feet, with long, streaming hair. *He's dressed casually and moves confidently.* He walks, with a long stride, straight toward Bob. *What does this guy want? Doesn't look like a crook.*

He's getting closer. Still doesn't look threatening. But he doesn't look friendly either. Indubitably, he has a muscular build and a downright broad and powerful frame. *Looks like he lifts a lot of heavy stuff.* His lips are set in a thin line. Up closer, it's obvious he also has cold, hard, calculating eyes and a formidable chin.

Within a stone's throw, he pauses a long time before speaking. When he does, he enunciates his words precisely, and his voice is like ice water. "My name's Malek," he says, with his hand extended.

Bob reciprocates, "I'm Bob Becker." The taller man sits down beside him without saying anything else. A hand benignly placed on Bob's forearm and soft-eyed contact suggests empathy.

In response, Bob looks out into space at nothing in particular. His face's washed clean of emotion. In a slow, somber voice, he tries to make conversation.

Randomly, he explains, "I was an orphan from birth." With that, he pauses.

Malek says nothing. In fact, he offers neither vocal nor physical response, not even a sigh or a nod of the head.

Bob continues slowly, "My first adopted father was Leonard Gilcrest. He was a cruel and abusive man. Can't count the number of whoopings he gave me."

Malek stares intently at him. His clear blue eyes seem to reach down into his soul.

"I remember," Bob states, "How he used to talk from the corner of his mouth." He stops and laughs briefly. "I don't recollect that nearly as well as I recall all the beatings. With a board, with a belt, or a tree branch, it didn't matter. He put his all into it." With that, Bob once again pauses. "Afterwards, he would lecture me in that high-pitched, squeaky voice of his. 'You know you have to learn from your mistakes,' he would say. 'You know you need to grow up. You need to be a man.'" Bob shutters as he wanders across the wild waste of years.

Malek looks deeply into Bob's eyes. For his part, Bob has a pained look on his face as he rubs his upper arms. The thought goes tripping through his mind: *I'm as muddled as a squirrel chasing a dog.* At last, he blurts out, *"Are you a ghost?"*

Bob Becker, High School Teacher

After a few minutes, as he looks the other way, Malek asks, "Howbeit, what about that day in Walmart?"

Pressing his fingers to his lips and then raking his hand through his hair, Bob repeats the question, "What happened in Walmart?" He pauses a moment before reflecting, "Dad kicked me right there in the aisle of the store. Folks were watching all around." Malek nods slightly. Chewing on his lower lip, Bob continues, "And this man I didn't know grabbed my Dad's arm. I heard him say, 'You put another hand on the boy, and I'll clean the floor up with you.' My Dad kept hands off, at least until we left the store. Never saw that man again."

Bob's memory scurries away to a place he'd rather it not go. Uninvited, the image stands before him, a man in his middle forties, tall and lanky, with brown hair streaked with gray.

Without real effort, Bob sees that wrinkled face, large nose, brown eyes, and a straggly mustache. What he remembers most about the man is that he was usually angry. *Even after all these years, I can still hear that clipped and curt voice.*

Bob's still engaged in unpleasant reverie when Malek says, "What about *thine* second stepfather?"

Bob makes the mental transition from personal abuse to awful neglect. Meandering into his recollections now is a man in his late thirties, on the pudgy side, with blond hair and a receding hairline. After all of these years, he's haunted by those blue eyes behind glasses sitting on a large hooked-nose. Clearly, he can hear that nasal voice saying, "No, I can't make your game. I've got work to do." *How often that phrase romps through my nightmares even after all of these years.*

Trying not to be rude, Bob asks, "Are you an apparition?"

After waiting several seconds, Malek says simply, "No."

Bob rubs the back of his head as he stares around him. Then he asks, "Why do you use so many archaic terms?"

With penetrating blue eyes, an extended chin, and a voice free of emotion, he admits, "I know 374 different languages, and all of them evolve over time. *Tis* hard to keep up with the *divers* expressions." He waits a moment, during which Bob's preparing to ask him some questions. Then, out of the blue, Malek says, "Forsooth, I am not a ghost, an elf, and while I'm at it, I am not human. I am not a goblin, a leprechaun, or the product of *beef-witted* human imagination. *Behold,* what I am is a celestial agent on assignment."

TWO:
A STRANGE ENCOUNTER

"My second adopted father, Simon Crenshaw, was an overachiever who was never available to me," explains Bob. "He always had stuff to do." With that, Bob goes silent.

Finally, Malek responds, "I *bethink* (remember) meeting him."

Bob's eyes blink as he answers, "Really?"

"But *heretofore* that is *nowise* what is bothering you now. Is it?"

Bob avoids looking at Malek, staring into space instead, as he says, "You know what, I don't know how to explain it, and you wouldn't understand it if I did."

Malek sits extremely still. He's expressionless and dispassionate as he makes very intensive eye contact. In a voice like ice water, he says, "*Forsooth,* I know fully the past. I understand what is happening in the present and what is yet to happen in the future. And, you think I cannot understand *aright* your feelings." He pauses a moment, then continues, "I can clearly apprehend how it bothers *thou* that you never knew your real father. *Aye,* you are also lamented *nowise* having a heritage to pass on to any of your future sons or daughters.

Often, you have beat your breast with the lamentation, "I'm going to die without ever knowing who I am or where I came from. That be why you are such a cranky pants."

As they stand to their feet, Bob stares at Malek's chiseled, defiant chin, jutting out like a unicorn's horn. His eyes are cold, hard, and calculating. Still, there's something about the man's face and his manner that tends to put Bob at ease. *Maybe, he's somebody who's seen too much and experienced too much.*

Malek announces, "You and I are about to take a trip. Through means of time manipulation, we're going to go back three hundred years."

Bob's stunned and completely at a loss for words. Going pale, he shakes his head. *Is this guy, whoever he is, out of his head?*

With a stoic facial expression and cold, hard, and calculating eyes, Malek rivets his eyes on Bob, giving him a piercing stare. His steely eyes seem to reach into the depths of his being. After a moment of mystifying silence, he states, "I know you think time is constant, but, *verily,* time is really an illusion. *Forsooth,* in this world, time depends on the spatial reference of the observer. Time travel, or time-shifting, is, *in truth,* achieved through the use of time dilation. *Howbeit,* it requires a large amount of energy, with which I have been equipped."

Bob's trying to wrap his head around what this character has said. He's being asked to believe two inconsistent things. Suspending his belief requires his prefrontal cortex to accept the reality of what he's hearing. He can't do it. Thus, the idea of time travel becomes only a string of words for him.

Through his superhuman intelligence, Malek slightly alters Bob's brain function. (The process is also called menticide.) Thus, he's transported, or at least partially transported, into an alternate reality.

Malek can now continue repeating himself, "Through means of time manipulation, we are going to go back in time three hundred years."

Leaning in with a slight smile, Bob inquires, "But why three hundred years?"

"My purpose," Malek explains, "Is to show you God has a long-term plan for your life. It extends from before this country came into being until today." He pauses a moment and then continues, "Three hundred is a tremendously important number. It's mentioned over thirty times in the Bible. I am sure you have read how Enoch walked with God after the birth of Methuselah for 300 years. Noah's Ark was 300 cubits long, Gideon defeated the Midianites with 300 men, and those are but a few. I will not mention its significance in history and science." He pauses a moment, then continues, "I personally find it interesting humans are born initially with three hundred bones and that nerve impulses travel 300 kilometers per hour through the human body."

Without saying a word, Malek takes him by the hand. "*Whithersoever*, we are about to make a trip," he declares solemnly. Then he takes his other hand.

THREE:
CAN THIS BE REAL?

Bob's taking short, shallow breaths. Avoiding eye contact, he looks at his hands and at the ground. There's small movement around his eyes and his lower lip's quivering. His mouth's getting dry, and he's grinding his teeth. His skin's crawling. Softly, he mouths, "Yikes."

A tremor of some kind is moving hurriedly up his arms. It feels like a hundred little pins are pricking his skin. *I can't see anything. I get vibes like I'm a kid again, whirling around and around on a playground merry-go-round. It's not like I'm falling; rather like I'm in an airplane, rolling over.* He's looking around, hoping to get his bearings. *What a shock!*

"Wow!" He's overwhelmed by what he sees. It's as unexpected as snow in summer. The park's gone; the ground's gone; the trees, once all around, are gone. *Where am I? Wherever it is, I'm moving through it really fast. Eye-blinking fast, streaking-star fast, tornadic wind fast. I'm moving unbelievably fast. Strange, there's no wind pressure against me.*

All of it stops. He's stationary once again. He's bewildered as he watches Malek. Specifically, he gives him the once-over as his clothes, his blue jeans and sweatshirt, give way to a long-sleeved shirt, knee-length breeches, and stockings.

Even more agog are the large buckles now appearing on both of his shoes. *Man, talk about weird.* By means of extrasensory perception, Malek knows what Bob's thinking.

In his head, not verbally, Malek says, "We have to fit in." The words are barely formed in his mouth, when Bob's own attire suddenly transforms. First, he loses his Nikkis, then his slacks, followed by his favorite pullover. In their place, he's now wearing clothes almost exactly like those on Malek.

Bob's flabbergasted. *What kind of fashion statement is this?* After smacking his forehead, he says, with his mouth open immensely, "Golly!" *Where did these clothes come from? How in the world did they get on me? Am I hallucinating? Am I losing my mind? This is another world.* Looking around, he ponders, *Unthinkable!*

While he hasn't said anything aloud, Malek responds. "You think I am a hallucination."

Malek, Special Agent

Bob answers, "I was just thinking..."

Malek looks toward the sky and slightly nods his head. With no inflection at all, he says, "You mean something like Personality Dissociative Disorder?"

Now befuddled, Bob's thinking is thrown off balance. He rapidly blinks his eyes before saying, "I think that sounds serious."

Malek takes a strong, erect stance with his hands on his hips. Then, in an even more inscrutable, matter-of-fact voice says, "Let's consider the symptoms. Anxiety? I don't see evidence of that. Well, maybe a little. Depression? Well, maybe a little. Drug abuse? No, I'm sure of that. Hallucinations? Hmmm." He puts two fingers to his lips before saying, "I'm real, and you are real. I hope you learn reality is all that exists. Memory variations? From what I see, you remember your past very clearly. Mood swings? Well, you are human, after all. Panic attacks? Again, I've seen you in stressful situations in which you completely control your emotions. What about the presence of two or more different personalities?

That one vanquishes the possibility. If you had another personality, I'm sure you would use it."

FOUR: ADVENTURE AHEAD

I'm on a bluff, overlooking what's probably a bay of some kind. He can see sun-drenched sand and calm, gentle waves. Three ships are docked at the harbor with their tall masts and riggings. One of them looks like it's being unloaded. Here and there, Bob recognizes dogwood clusters of tiny green flowers. Their aroma is sweet and floral. They smell like honey-suckle or jasmine. With a little twisting and turning, he notices a few Redbud trees with vibrant pink flowers. A coastal sea breeze carries a salty scent. *This sure ain't Texas.*

Along the side of the road are Joe-pye weeds, rounded clusters of pink flowers, with a fragrance like vanilla. On the spot, he hears, "Kaw," and "Kaaaw." Looking up, he sees seagulls making that harsh, distinctive call.

Looking around him, at a handful of multicolored row-houses, the cobble-stone street, and the quaint, antique-looking streetlamp. He asks, "Where are we, anyway?"

Malek walks with an erect posture and long steps. He lacks any facial expression. Nothing to indicate emotion, no sign of inner feelings, making him appear composed and even apathetic. After a moment, he says, "*Forsooth,* we are in the Colony of Virginia. It is a business enterprise of…"

Bob interrupts him, "The English Trading Company."

Malek replies, "Well, you do know your history. This year is 1724. *Be-think* (remember). The colony was chartered by English King James VI, the same man who authorized the King James translation of the Bible. *Verily,* this is also the year the glass thermometer is invented."

Without notice, Malek changes the seriousness of his monologue. "Kidnapped Africans were brought here for the first time a little over a hundred years ago. Today, slavery is thoroughly entrenched in all thirteen colonies. An estimated 75,000 black people are now enslaved in this colony. The total population, all together, is a little over two million."

The dialogue changes direction as Malek points out four oxen pulling a wagon, approaching them. He calls to Bob's attention, the teamster, a black man, walking on the nearside (left). "You know they're called 'bull-wackers.'" Bob's intrigued, wonderstruck actually, at the large animals, two are reddish brown, one gray, and the other black. Even though the squeaking wagon is heavily loaded, they're plugging along at more than five miles per hour. Malek jumps in with, "Oxen pull heavier loads than horses or donkeys, even though they're slower." As the driver yells, "Haw," the transport team turns right and moves down a different street. As they move away, Malek adds, "When the oxen reach age seven, they're sold for beef."

After pausing a moment, possibly to see if Bob has anything to say, Malek offers, "*Heretofore,* Pennsylvania is the fastest growing of all the Thirteen colonies. Two years ago, South Carolina became a Royal Colony. The period is characterized by conflict between ..."

Speaking over him, Bob completes the sentence, "Between the French, English and Spanish colonies." Then, with a sigh conveying arrogance, he continues, "You know I teach history." His pace takes a slight but brief strut or swagger.

Malek is completely aware of their surroundings. Still, he decides not to warn Bob of the one-horse carriage approaching them at a fast clip. It's actually a one-horse roadster. Of course, Malek knows very well the man driving the two-wheel buggy. His name is Dexter deBaugh, tobacco farmer. He's of average height, heavy-set, two degrees past pudgy. The self-important man's bald, though he frequently wears a white wig, especially when in public, such as today. He has full cheeks, a bulbous nose, and excessively full eyebrows.

"Hey!" Bob yells, jumping out of the way. "Why don't you watch where you're going, fellow!" Bob's irritation is almost choking him. It rushes through him.

Two blocks farther down the street, again they meet Mister deBaugh. Bob doesn't recognize him, but he realizes who they are. A fresh swell of anger rises in de Baugh, With a strident and unpleasant voice, he snarls, "Thou be-est the idiot who walketh in the middle of the street."

Bob starts to respond, "And you. . ." *I'm gonna tell this idiot off.*

Malek nods his head, giving Bob a silent warning. In a voice as soft as rain, he whispers, "This isn't our fight."

Using deductive logic, Bob reasons, *"This isn't our fight," suggests that something or someone will be our fight.* He licks his lips and rubs his hands together. A flood of excited energy floods through him. He's bubbling with enthusiasm, this is apparent through his gestures and his facial expressions. *Now, there's so much to see, so much to do. Adventure is ahead.* He jerks his fist down. *It's as if a storm cloud is opening up over me.* A whole different level of expectation envelopes him.

Belinda, Bob's Fiancé

FIVE:
WHO IS RYAN LOGAN?

Out of the blue, Malek says, "There's someone I want you to meet." Bob's lost in thought. *I'm sure he's about to introduce me to someone from my past. That means I'll get some of my questions answered. I bet he's somebody with a brilliant mind. Perhaps, he's somebody who changed history in some way. Wouldn't that be something?*

Without warning, in front of them, down the street, an informal crowd has gathered. They aren't angry. On the contrary, everyone appears joyfully excited.

A well-dressed man, with a pronounced English accent is saying, "Now, Thomas, how many seconds are in a year and a half?"

A young, shirtless, black teenager, looks bewildered at the crowd. Then he says, "Forty-seven thousand, three hundred and four."

The Englishman, addressing the crowd, says, "And, he can't read or write."

The crowd, "Oos" and, "Awes."

The Englishman starts again, "A man has lived seventy years, seventeen days, and twelve hours. How many seconds has he lived?"

Almost immediately, the young man says, "Two billion, two hundred ten million, five hundred thousand, eight hundred." One of the men in the crowd is busy with a fountain pen and a tablet. After several minutes, the man admits, "That's exactly right." Everyone, including Bob, is astonished.

Bob looks at Malek quizzically. He says nothing Bob's expecting. Instead, he takes him by the arm and leads him away. Bob's reluctant. "That young man's a mental calculator."

Malek continues pulling him away as Bob asks, "Who is he? I wanted to meet him." After they have progressed a ways, Malek explains, "That young man's Thomas Fuller. He was kidnapped in Africa and brought here, and he's about to be sold as a slave. I didn't want to watch the sale, and I didn't think you would either."

Bob responds, "You're so right about that."

Malek follows with, "I suppose you aren't interested in going to the fields where people work from sunup to sunset?" Bob doesn't reply. "You could see why life expectancy this year is fifty-six," Malek says.

The two of them continue their stroll down the dirt and cobblestone road, that will one day become King Street. *The weather is so different here. Indeed. The muggy sky can't decide if it wants to rain or not.* The sultry weather soaks into their bones. It's hard for Bob to believe how clammy and oppressive it is.

Approaching them from the opposite direction, walking slowly but deliberately, is a tall young man. He appears muscular and his dark brown hair is worn long. Bob pays him no mind, but Malek takes note of his beard and mustache. As he gets closer, Malek stops and says, "Excuse me, sir, can you tell us a good place to eat lunch?"

The man replies empathetically, "You might try the tavern over yonder. It's the best place there is for miles."

With that, Bob starts to walk away, but he stops when Malek asks the stranger, "You are Ryan Logan, aren't you?"

The stranger is taken aback. "Yes, I am," he admits. With raised eyebrows, he enquires, "Do I know you?"

Malek maintains a straight face saying, "Probably not, but we have heard of you." He suddenly becomes joyful as a bubbling creek or as a wave dancing in the sea. A slow smile spreads over his thin lips. With a satisfied look on his face, Ryan walks away. When he's out of earshot, Malek tells Bob, "You just met one of your ancestors twenty-eight generations back."

SIX:
EAVESDROPPING IN A TAVERN

Bob stops dead in his tracks. He's blown away by Malek's identifying one of his ancestors. Laughter shows on his face. Malek takes note of his wrap-around smile and how he starts swinging his arms while walking.

As they approach one of the taverns, Bob notices a sign in front, "The Pig and the Carrot."

That's weird. Making conversation again, Malek remarks, "*Howbeit,* did you know there are one hundred of these taverns in Philadelphia?" Bob gives a one-shoulder shrug in response.

In a matter-of-fact way, Malek continues, "Forty percent of all taverns are operated by women, usually widows." Bob sloughs off a hint of a shrug.

Inside the tavern, a totally different atmosphere confronts them. The air's filled with a hodgepodge of aromas. The place reeks of the smell of smoke, food, and body sweat. All classes of people, seamen, laborers, and plantation owners, are here. In the large taproom are tables, an extra-large bar, and a huge fireplace crackling opposite the bar. A quick glance reveals not only does this tavern serve as a gathering place, but also as a convenience store of sorts. A dozen or so men are drinking at the bar, and about the same number are playing cards. The only women in the place are dancing with three scruffy and grungy-looking men. In one corner, two men are fighting. It's not much of a ruckus. In all probability, both men are too drunk for a bona fide battle.

They sit down at the long food table. *Everything smells good.* Different types of roast meat are available. There are also cucumbers, cabbage, and carrot puffs, similar to hush puppies. Bob's trying to decide between Gooseberry pie or rice pudding when he develops an interest in a nearby conversation. The chat's taking place at the bar, but he can't make out what they're saying. One of those men is Dexter deBaugh. Bob's annoyed by the loud and boisterous tone of their dialogue. *Those two creeps could at least dial the volume down a little.*

Noticing his interest, Malek poses the question, "How do you feel about eavesdropping?"

Bob nods his head in their direction and responds, "From here?"

Malek replies, "I can hear those skilamalinks, and their secret, shady discussion." In the voice of Dexter deBaugh, Malek says, "My three-year contract with Ryan Logan is up this week. I need est him to make my crop."

His companion's another planter, judging by his attire. He responds, "I don't see the problem. Indentured servants are the same as slaves; you have to treat them the same way. It happens all the time. If he gives you any trouble, put the hammer down."

SEVEN:
SKIPPING A WEEK

Malek places a hand on Bob's hand. He looks deep into his eyes as he says, "Let's skip ahead a week or so." There's no fanfare, no lights flashing, and no weird or eerie sounds. One moment, they're here; the next, they're gone.

Bob can't believe his eyes. It isn't the transition that shocks him, nor is it their new location that amazes him. He's stunned to see twenty-seven year old, Ryan Logan, being locked in stocks. Three men are brutally latching his ankles between two boards. Next, they bind his hands the same way. His face is scrunched with pain and anguish. His left eye is black and swollen closed. With his other eye, he's gazing downward and to the side. His face is pale and bruised.

Unnecessarily, Malek explains, "The purpose of this brand of punishment is humiliation." There's no doubt about the effectiveness of this cruelty.

Bob scrutinizes the bruises on his ancestor's face, his shoulders, and back. Revulsion sweeps over him. One eyebrow raises. With a grudging tone, he snarls, "Who does that scum bag think he is?"

Several other people come by with lips pursed to one side, no doubt expressing disapproval, or smirking, or sneering. Others show their reproof by shaking their heads. Bob's irritated in the extreme. *I'd like to slap all their faces.*

He looks at Ryan empathetically. "What happened to you?"

For a moment, Ryan just sits there with his eyes closed. Then he explains, "The bottom fact is I messed up. It all started with a man named John Rolfe. He was a captain who brought a sweet tobacco seed from Trinidad, in the Caribbean. Selling those seeds was under penalty of death by the Spanish. Even so, he brought them here and planted them. From his plantation, he exported this new tobacco back to Britain. It became an instant hit. Then, he married Pocahontas, who converted to Christianity. Back in Britain, he wrote a book about how tobacco plantations in the New World were going to be so profitable." Bob's fingers go to his mouth in contemplation as he listens.

At this moment, Malek adds, "In August, of 1610, the first shipload of slaves were sold here in this Colony. Now, there are blacks from Africa, Native Indians, and white slaves."

Bob nods in understanding.

Ryan takes up his story again. "When I heard in London, that men could make a fortune here, I decided that was for me. I'm not bottled-headed (void of wit). Trouble was, it was too high for my nut." Bob looks confused. Ryan continues, "It was beyond my reach." Bob leans toward him and makes soft eye contact with him.

Ryan rolls his eyes. Shaking his head, he goes stone-faced. With a pained expression, he explains, "My indenture contract was up last week. I went in and said, 'Good-bye' to deBaugh. He became angry, saying. 'the Indenture Contract you signed before leaving England stipulates you must serve ten years. That wasn't true; I read it myself. When I tried to leave, he charged me as a run-away. So, here I am."

Confused, Bob asks, "Why did he do that?"

Ryan responds, "Damfino (short for "Damned if I know)."

With his head back and his chin thrust forward, Malek watches passionlessly as Bob loses his cool. A swell of rage is rising in his face, and it's about to burst within him. Resentment is growing mightily in him like a supersonic tumor. Malek does nothing to tamp down the irritation he sees vibrating in the younger man. In fact, it amuses him to watch him breathing hard and blowing out his cheeks.

"What do we do?" Bob asks, "We can't let this stand." He looks at Malek, searching for an answer.

Ryan's mouth is pulled downward, his lips are quivering, and his shoulders are slumped.

Malek, unruffled, declares, "*For soothe*, you two need to cheer up. Your Father's still in charge. Bob, you stay here and get to know Ryan better. *Verily*, I'll be back in a few minutes."

Trying to make conversation and hoping to learn something about his ancestor, Bob asks,

"What's it like on a tobacco plantation?"

With repressed anger, Ryan's disturbed and even a bit physically ill. He mutters under his breath, "I got nothing more to say." Later, when he does decide to speak, he spits out his words with contempt, his voice rising as he does. His face is hardening, and his teeth are grinding. "Life on a tobacco plantation is pretty grim since the price of tobacco fell like a rock two years ago." Suddenly, an awful scowl rolls across his face. An unsuppressed tear rolls down his face.

On the spot, Ryan's demeanor changes. Turning around, Bob is surprised to see Dexter deBaugh. The man's in his mid-forties; short and overweight. *Reminds me of my first stepfather. Course my Dad didn't have a straggly mustache, like this dufus.* Bob stares at the belligerent face before him, thinking, *That wig's got to be the dumbest looking thing ever.*

The chubby man's mouth is slightly open on one side. One eyebrow rises, and his nose wrinkles. "What are you doing here talking to my slave?" he demands. The man's displeasure looks like it's almost choking him. When speaking, it's easy to hear mounting exasperation tightening in his throat. "You need to get your butt out of here," he rants.

EIGHT:
A COWBOY NEEDS A HORSE

The thought comes tripping through Bob's mind, *I'm going to show this creep.* What he says is, "I was just making conversation."

With fire in his eyes, deBaugh roars, "People like you are dumb as dirt."

Bob comes back with, You should be ashamed of yourself for treating people like this."

Hearing that, he draws back preparing to hit Bob.

Bob turns around quickly. In the blink of an eye, he slams his fist into the man's face. CLUNK! FA-THUD. Mister Pudgy hits the ground.

Rubbing his jaw and groaning, he's dazed. With great effort, after a while he manages to get up. Massaging his chin, he looks back and forth and makes guttural throat sounds. In a higher-pitched voice, he yells, "I'll be back. We'll take care of you!" With that, he walks away swiftly, imitating a run.

A look of satisfaction captures Bob's face. Ryan groans, "He'll be back with a dozen men."

Bob tries to readjust his own thinking. For a good while, he tries to encourage Ryan and lift his spirits. *Not many people are on the street this morning. The air's crisp and the sun's shining gloriously. The sky awoke in a good mood this morning, and it looks like it will hold all day.* But, he's unable to calm the apprehension growing in his gut. Adrenaline spikes and his mouth gets dry. Goosebumps start forming on his arms.

Suddenly, his apprehension turns to panic. Two blocks away, deBaugh is running toward him. A pack of rowdy men are running with him toward them. They're loud and raucous as they hoot and howl. Even from here he can tell they're armed with sticks, pistols and long knives. He doesn't have to struggle to figure out what they've got on their minds.

Bob looks around, hoping to see Malek. Alas, he's nowhere to be seen. Bob has a shortness of breath and his muscles are twitching. Without further to do, reluctantly he starts running. *Which way?*

To the wharf? To the taverns? He runs toward some houses. Taking a momentary refuge in an outdoor kitchen, he asks himself, *What do I do now?*

That very minute, he sees Malek, only two blocks away. He's on horseback. A gasp of surprise escapes him. *What in the world is he doing horse-back riding?* As the mounted Malek gets close, Bob eases up close to him. Looking over the horse's rump, he's shocked.

He can't believe his eyes. *There's no reason for their behavior. DeBaugh* and his friends turn down a side street and move hurriedly away from them.

He exhales a huge pent-up breath. Smiling broadly, he says, "Whew!" Sincere thankfulness runs through his mind. He looks up at Malek and says, "Boy, am I glad you're here."

As they get nearer to Ryan, Bob studies the horse a little closer. The horse looks to be eleven to twelve hands high. It's chocolate-colored, with no white markings. Looks like he can give a comfortable ride for long distances.

NINE:
INTO ANOTHER WORLD

Bob joins Malek as he returns to where Ryan sits in stocks. With no explanations, apology, or encouragement, Malek turns the mechanism's lock to soft pudding. With his thumb and one finger, he pulls the lock apart. He then pushes the restraining board up, freeing Ryan. Bob helps Ryan to his feet. The lock securing Ryan's feet is disposed of just as quickly. Malek then says, "Hold your hand out." When he does, Malek drops six gold nuggets in that hand, saying, "These are for you."

Horizontal wrinkle lines form on his forehead, and his jaw drops. His eyes are big and wide.

Malek dismisses his surprise by saying, "It's *naught*; I picked those up on the side of the road *whence* I come from." Bob's upper eyelids also rise as his eyes widen. He marvels even more at what Malek says next. "This *steed* is a gift to you from Bob and I. We *sorely* suggest you take the gold and the *steed* and get out of town quickly, *whithersoever* as you can. It would most probably be *meet* to go into the frontier."

The first thing Ryan says is, "Yahoo, yeehaw!" the next thing he says is, "Thank you, both." He wastes no time mounting the horse and riding away at a gallop. "Gallopity-glop, clippity-clop!" Malek and Bob stand, watching him ride away.

"*Ye* know we aided and abetted a man breaking the law," Malek declares. Even as he raises the question, he appears detached and inscrutable.

As they stroll along, Bob casually mentions, "Ever notice how some trees have a sweet smell, and others have a sour or bitter smell. For example, Douglas fir smells like grapefruit, and Balsam Poplar smells like sweet honey in the spring." With his shoulders upright and slightly aback and a slight smile, he looks at Malek.

Malek moves with a determined, purposeful walk using large steps. His face is stony and remote. His voice is unemotional. "Do *thou* smell those trees here? Or, *mayhaps* are you trying to impress me?"

Blushing, Bob admits, "Neither, just trying to make conversation while I try to figure out how to tell you deBaugh is coming after me. And I want to ask you if we can see how Ryan turns out—in a hurry."

Malek repeats the question as though he hasn't heard him. "How does Ryan do on the frontier?"

Bob declares simply, "That's right."

TEN:
DOWN AN OLD WAGON ROAD

Without so much as a head turn, Malek replies, "Place-shifting and time shifting can nowise be achieved without the help of a facilitator."

With a measure of irritability, Bob replies, "Yes, I know; you have already told me that."

Malek's response is, "Let's go see anon." They join hands as a precursor to time travel. Before beginning the process, Malek says, "*Afore* we go, let me remind you not to do *aught* that might jeopardize his future and/or your past. *Howbeit*, let us try six years into the future."

The journey's faster than a tripped man falling. It's also relatively routine for Malek. But Bob's still filled with amazement at the improbable event. The willies are with him an hour later. As their feet settle in place, Bob's astonished. Stepping into another new world, he starts bouncing around and clapping his hands. His eyes are wide open. The ground beneath their feet is different. It's rocky and hard. And rocks? Rough, giant, irregular boulders and pebbles are everywhere. The air's also different. It's cooler and there's a pronounced aroma of fir trees in it. And the scenery's definitely different. Towering trees are everywhere, mostly oaks and beeches, mixed in with firs. Mountains, in rows and rows, are majestic and mysterious. Soft and wispy mist ascends behind each ridge. Massive tan rocks, bespeckled with white blotches, stand guard over the hillsides. Here and there are clumps of magenta-colored flowers.

With little inflection, Malek explains, "*Forsooth*, they be rhododendrons."

The two of them are walking down a seldom-traveled, dusty road. Actually, it amounts to kindred paths forming a wagon road. Fifty yards to their left is a small stream. The burbling, cascading brook is splashing and trilling as it threads through rocks. Watching it and listening to it helps lighten the mood. It even makes Bob feel peaceful. He says, "Being here makes you appreciate how short life is."

They've walked a ways in silence when Malek solemnly says, "*Behold*, we have experienced time contraction thither (toward) a settlement on the *tother* side of Appalachian Mountains. *Heretofore*, most of the settlers *heretofore* were involved in the fur business."

Arriving at a small log cabin, snuggled against a rock wall, Bob exclaims, "Doesn't look like Ryan's doing too well." The cabin isn't a shack, but it isn't more than a couple of degrees beyond. Little more than ten by ten, it has a single window and an animal skin for a front door. Chinking between the logs has deteriorated and needs repair. As they get closer, they meet the owner. Turns out, the resident is an overweight man wearing a leather, buckskin shirt, with a long fringe. In addition, he has a broken nose and two missing teeth.

He introduces himself as Earni Smith, somewhat guardedly. They ask him if he knows Ryan Logan.

Stuttering, he replies, "This here used to be his p-p-place; built it when he f-f-first got here. Four years ago, he married an Indian girl, and they b-b-built a larger cabin downstream beside the creek."

The two of them casually make their way to the Logan's homestead. The fragrant rustle of leaves underfoot comforts them both. Malek explains, "*Methinks nature's whispering to us from among the leaves.*" From some distance away, they're able to see the cabin and tendrils of ash-colored smoke rising from their chimney.

ELEVEN:
COUNTRY LIFE ON THE FRONTIER

The place's rugged but rustic. It's a log cabin but it has a wide porch, extending across the front. It also has two dogs of unidentifiable breed cavorting in the front yard. They're playing with a little boy. The cute child has sandy brown hair and more energy than seems possible. He's running and jumping all over the place. As soon as he sees them, he runs back inside.

Within minutes, his mother comes out. She's a beautiful young lady, of the girl next door type. She has dark, smoldering eyes and high cheekbones. She also has pitch-black, long, waist-length hair, woven into braids. A narrow, white loop is wrapped around her head. Her beige-colored leather dress has long, full sleeves, with unbelievably long fringe. Seeing the two men, she turns and hollers, "Ryan, come!"

When he appears in the doorway, Bob's surprised at how different he now looks. His dark brown hair, which was long before, is now closely cropped. And, he no longer has a beard or mustache. Nevertheless, his fence post teeth remain. Of course, he still has the dark spot under his left eye. Those brown eyes now have web-like wrinkles around them. It's clear he has definitely aged, his face is seamed with lots of lines and a somewhat weather-beaten appearance. *Yeah, he's still raw-boned and lean with a gaunt frame.*

Ryan can hardly believe his eyes. He's bowled over and speechless. Finally, he says, "Well, I'll be a monkey's uncle!" In addition, he's stunned that Bob and Malek look just as they did six years earlier. A comet of joy streaks through him as he starts laughing, giggling, and dancing around. Rushing towards them, he grabs and hugs each one. "Boy, am I glad to see you," he says gleefully. "Come and meet my wife," he invites as he pulls them toward her. "This is Teata, my wonderful wife."

She hugs each of them, saying, "Ryan say much about you. Welcome to our home."

The little boy's tugging on her and she lifts him. Dancing drops of joy are in her eyes as she announces, "This be Delano, our son." Bob and Malek immediately agree that the little fellow is precious. He's also pudgy, with blue eyes. When his mother puts him down, they decide he's also extremely energetic.

Appalachian Home of Ryan and Teata

Bob asserts, "Ryan, we're so glad to see you again." As he does, he breaks out in laughing and giggling. It occurs to him, *Can't think of a time when I've been more glad? Dopamine are certainly at work in me.*

Bereft of singing or humming, as well as any dancing around, Malek offers, "*Verily*, it looks like you're doing really well. *Forsooth*, look at this place, a nice house, a corral full of animals, a beautiful wife, and fabulous surroundings." His rock-hard chin is slightly tilting as he speaks. But he's free of any emotion, or at least that's what his face suggests. He actually isn't distant or cold, however, this is the impression one gets watching him. For this reason, Teata's perplexed. Her forehead wrinkles as questions romp through her mind. Bob picks up on her confused look. *She'll get used to his ways as she gets to know him.* He also notes, *There's a uniqueness to her scent. It's earthy yet delicious. Wonder what it is?*

With a glowing smile, she says to Ryan, "Why you no bring out stools." With that, he gives her a soft, gentle touch and retreats inside. She follows him. In a moment, he's back with two hand-made wooden stools. They're actually carved from hackberry, which still has a fresh, green aroma. In a flash, she brings out the third stool and motions for them to be seated. In nothing flat, the three of them are deep in conversation, prattling away like lifelong friends. Ryan tells them about his beaver trapping, about his wife's garden, and about South Carolina becoming a state last year.

Bob mentions they have seen Ryan's earlier house and says, "You definitely did a lot better on this one. It looks great."

Impassive, with no hint of feeling, Malek asserts, "Ryan, I am really proud of you. *Betimes* (in a short time), you have done really well." There's a strong note of earnestness in his voice.

Inside the cabin, they sit on the same stools at a hand-made wooden table. The plates are hand-carved wood, as are the spoons. Turns out, Teata is a fabulous cook. The venison tastes like roast beef, while the potatoes, from her own garden, are delicious. Mustard greens, even though Bob can't identify them as such, taste sweet, spicy and tremendous. The mouth-watering meal makes all of them feel good. The table talk is mutually nurturing and uplifting. Even so, Bob's dumbfounded to hear Malek say, "*Betwixt* me and thee, Ryan, I believe in you and hope you believe in yourself as much as I do."

During dessert, a delicious blackberry pudding, Bob scrutinizes the interior of the Logan home. The simple one-room house is strangely roomy. The fireplace, and the fire therein, are mesmerizing to him. The birch wood, burning there, has a pleasant smell, not too smokey or strong. It provides an inviting atmosphere. *I can imagine curling up by this fire with Belinda, enjoying its warmth on a chilly evening.* The image of her comes skipping into his mind.

Those eyes, blue as ice, are sparkling. Her face is lit up. She smiles, with her lips, her eyes, and her heart. Suddenly, he's forced back to reality.

The windows, he is told, are made of paper, greased with animal fat, which makes them waterproof and translucent. The place is well-lighted, and judging by all the lanterns and candles, it's well-lit at night as well. The broad ax and the bowl-maker adze, hanging on the wall, aren't Bob's idea of room décor. The dirt floor and the absence of bathroom facilities also aren't that inviting. Still, the place is warm and inviting. *And it's scrupulously clean.*

During the course of their meal, Teata, Ryan's wife, is exuberant, nodding and laughing during the chit-chat. Joy's sparkling inside her. It shows in little ways. She uses endearing names for her husband and son, some of which he doesn't understand. She sees to it everyone's needs are met. And she hums as she moves about the cabin. Bob's captivated by the interaction between Ryan and his wife. *My ancestors certainly have a good relationship with each other.* A smile plays across his face, thinking about that. *At least that's a heritage of some kind.*

Teata

As Ryan is explaining to Malek how he used saddle notches to put the oak logs together building the cabin. Malek asserts, "The population in the thirteen colonies is doubling every generation." Bob's musing, *How would Belinda and I like living here? It's so isolated.*

There's no doubt these two are happy here. She has a wrap-around smile. He concludes they're rapturous. He's kind to others, he seems to be self-confident, and he's doing things he enjoys. In fact, they seem to be as happy as a clam at high water.

As they finish dinner, Ryan insists on showing them his tobacco crop and his tobacco barn.

TWELVE: HOME IN APPALACHIA

After the grand tour, they're once again sitting on the porch, listening to Teata singing inside. Bob's moved by her singing though he understands none of it. "Ta ray sum mo lu." Her voice has a lilt that makes Bob think of butterflies and tinkling bells. The dying day is whispering goodbye as the sun drifts to the west.

Bob's relaxing with his arms behind his head, lost in thought. He flirts with the idea of what his wedding day and his wedding night might be like. He stares at the burbling stream and the water bouncing off the rocks. He listens with fascination to the constant gurgling.

On the spur of the moment, Malek lifts his chin and tilts his head to one side. His lips are set in a thin line. As per usual, he has a stoic or blank facial expression.

Bob picks up on his sudden movement. *What's going on?* In a softened voice tone, he asks him, "What is it?" Bob's accustomed to him pausing a long time before speaking, so it isn't particularly troubling that he remains silent.

Malek's normal audacious blue eyes now become cold, hard, and calculating, like shark eyes. He stands quickly to his feet. Immediately, he strides away with strong, even steps. He moves in a power walk, with his big shoulders leaning from side to side. His muscles ripple as he walks. Within seconds, he disappears down the road.

Ryan's anxious as a tingling moves over him. He clears his throat and glances around, for what? He isn't sure. He looks stiff and uncomfortable as he asks, "Has Malek left us?"

Bob reassures him. "Of course not. He had something he had to do." Running through his mind is the thought. *I wish I knew what he had to do in such a hurry.* After a few minutes, some errant thoughts intrude into his thinking. *What if something happens and Malek doesn't or can't come back? How would I get home? Why didn't he tell me where he was going? What's going on?*

THIRTEEN: WHERE HAS OUR PROTECTOR GONE?

There and then, Delano comes running out of the door. Teata's right behind him. Both are giggling and laughing. The little game of chase continues across the front yard, with the two dogs joining in.

Bob jumps to his feet, saying, "I bet I can catch that boy." With that, he scampers about playfully, with his arms outstretched. Of course, he pretends to fail in his effort for a while. Then, he scoops up the boy and hugs him close. Both his Mom and Dad look on with satisfaction. The dos have no comment.

All of sudden, Teata remarks, "What's that?" She's pointing down the road. An eerie red glow appears near the horizon. Everyone stares at this new baffling mystery. It quickly becomes apparent that a cloud of fire is rising from the ground. "Something on fire," Teata declares.

But there's something else.

Within seconds, here comes Malek up the road. He's running at full tilt. His long hair's waving in the wind. He's moving with hurried, long steps. With him, Earnie Smith's struggling to keep up. All three of them near the cabin anxiously fix their gaze upon the two running men.

As the runners get closer, they notice Earnie's chest is heaving rapidly in heavy panting.

He looks like a dog after a chase. He can't talk when he reaches them. Malek voluntarily stays silent. All eyes are on Earnie. His chest heaves rapidly, with urgent gasps.

Wheezing, he pulls in a lung full of air with quick snatches. Finally, he's able to say, "T-t-t-that's…that's...my house."

Fierce flames are soon soaring over the tree line. The blaze casts a glow on the horizon. The conflagration is growing. Everyone's full of questions, "What started it?"

"What should we do about it?" and, "How did Earnie get away?"

Malek ignores all their questions. He's in a frenzy. Hurriedly and irrationally, he tries to usher them into the house.

Their eyes bore into him. Bob's asking, "Are you sure," while Ryan's at a loss for words.

Earnie's shaking his head.

In a matter-of-fact tone, he pronounces, "Get inside, *anon*, lock the door, and close the shutters on the windows." Without questions or hesitation, they get inside. Once inside, everyone grabs a weapon. Ryan has his long rifle. Earnie has a flintlock pistol in his right hand, Teata has a knife, and Bob has the broad ax off the wall. Malek remains outside.

Earnie asks the obvious question, "Why doesn't Malek come inside?"

Malek sits down coolly on the porch.

Indoors, all three adults either freeze in place or have stiffened movements. Adrenaline spikes all around. Bob notices he has clammy hands. Looking through a small peephole in a window shutter, Teata is whispering a prayer. Ryan leans his rifle against the wall and rubs the crawling skin on his arms. Earnie wishes he could run and hide.

FOURTEEN: GRAMY AND GRUBBY

Several tense minutes have passed. Malek casually stands to his feet in front of the porch. His feet are spread, and his hands are on his hips. Totally composed, he holds his chin high. His head is back in emblematic defiance.

Inside, looking through a crack, Bob's asking himself, *What now? What does Malek see?*

A solitary man ambles up in the yard in front of the house. He has rambled over from across the stream. The man's wearing a large, black, broad-brimmed hat. He's beefy. A bit more and he would be flabby. He's also totally unkempt. His buckskin shirt is grimy and grubby. Worse, his face and hands look as though they haven't been washed all week. On his left side, Chubby has an ax tucked through his belt. On his right side is a long knife in a holster. With a one-sided contempt smile, he says, "Comment allez-vous, mona mi?" ("How are you doing, my friend?")

Malek's impassive, no hint of feelings whatever. His chin's chiseled. His eyes, normally blue as a hummingbird, are dead like doll eyes. In a voice like ice water, in French, he says, "What can I do for you, you murderer?"

Inside the cabin, Bob picks up on the French word *meurtrie're*. He lets out a gasp of surprise. Horizontal wrinkle lines appear on his forehead. *What's Malek doing?* A questioning look appears on his face. *Why is he insulting a total stranger?*

FIFTEEN:
INSULTING A FRENCHMAN

A swell of rage is now rising in the face of the unkempt, chubby Frenchman. Angry words flow out of him like lava. "Desole', en bas, belelle!" (You sorry, low-down weasel.)

His red face looks like he's going to explode. He nervously transfers his weight from one leg to another and back again.

Malek remains aloof. He continues to stand stoically, without saying a word. His silence is interpreted as arrogance by the short visitor, and that increases his irritation.

Inside the cabin, words are exchanged in whispers. Earnie mouths, "We're in trouble now." Mounting exasperation tightens in his throat, almost choking him.

Ryan asserts quietly, "We're already having trouble with the French. This can't be good." He and Teata exchange looks with each other. Unspoken is the nervous sense of foreboding they both feel.

Bob comes out with, "Malek knows what he's doing." At the same time, he thinks, *I hope he knows.*

Teata announces, "Look!" What she sees is two Indians approaching the stocky man.

Following closely behind them is another white man. He's wearing a coonskin cap. It's hard to tell where the cap ends and his grungy beard starts. The Indians are dressed pretty much like the white man, with faded shirts and pants, plus dark coats. They have no feathers and no war paint.

Ryan declares loudly, "They're Choctaw Indians!"

Earnie Smith opens, "They're flatheads, alright."

Bob's bewildered. His thinking processes are on strike. "What do you mean they're flatheads?"

Teata supplies the answers, "Choctaws put pressure on baby heads and little children to make heads flat."

One of the Indians is carrying a Charlesville musket, a standard French issue, just like that carried by the Frenchman confronting Malek. The second Choctaw is armed with a bow and a quiver full of arrows. That very minute, he's nocking an arrow to his bow.

He's about to draw that bow.

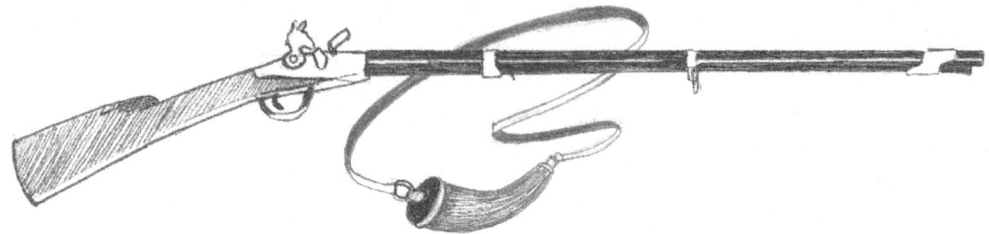

Charlesville .69 Caliber, French Musket

SIXTEEN:
SLOWLY FLYING ARROW

With cold, hard, calculating eyes, Malek stares at the man. Then he does a bit of space-time manipulation, or as it's known among men of science, *Chronokinesis*. What happens is he bends time in order to control it without affecting the flow of time generally.

As it is seen through Malek's eyes, the man draws his bow like pomegranate syrup in the wintertime. It moves through the air snail-like. Malek reaches up and grabs it tortoise-like.

As everyone else hears what is too fast to see. "Twang," the arrow leaves the bow.

"Swoosh," the arrow's flying through the air as fast as the speed of light. "Thwoot," Malek catches the arrow in his hand faster than a hummingbird's wing. The Indian's jaw goes slack. A questioning look takes over his face. He's muddled as a squirrel chasing a dog.

Everyone's amazed. They shake their heads, being at a total loss for words. The truth is, no one believes it. That is, until, after holding the arrow a moment, Malek breaks the arrow and throws both parts to the ground.

The overall situation now goes from bad to worse. They're up to their necks in trouble.

In the cabin, they're dumbfounded. More than a dozen more Choctaws shuffle up like a coyote walking past a henhouse. Two of them are carrying torches. They now surround the cabin.

A sense of foreboding is growing inside. All three adults look stiff and uncomfortable.

Teata's trembling and wringing her hands. An unquenchable fire has spread from a house fire to a forest fire. A wall of flames, though some distance away, is growing. The acrid taste of smoke is growing even in the cabin.

Malek keeps a steady eye on the changing situation. Humans wouldn't have the intellectual capacity to handle all of these multiple threats at one time. By contrast,

Malek's intelligence far surpasses that of the most gifted and brightest humans. Right now, requiring more concentration than other things, is the two Indians carrying torches.

Both flames flicker and dance. The situation is spine-chilling. Bob ponders. *It's still not dark enough for normal torch use. Why have they lit them? What will Malek do about this?*

Actually, he can already feel the energy he has summoned flowing into his eyes.

Using that energy, he creates an electrical ray flying from his brain to his two opponents' motor cortex (a thin strip on the top of a brain). They are physically or mentally unable to resist.

Agony is written on both their faces. They grit their teeth, trying to resist. Both faces twist as they fight to overcome their imprisoned mind. Still, they throw their torches into the stream. They sizzle, as they go out, is warmly welcome in the cabin.

The chubby Frenchman's rage is now exploding. His fists are clenched. Pronounced vertical wrinkles appear between his eyes. His nostrils flare.

The evening sun, the slow-crawling, apricot orange colored, is setting in the west. Cool-headed, Malek declares, "*So be it.* Everyone stay inside, no matter what!"

Inside, locked and bolted, everyone finds their opening, a hole or a crack through which they can watch what's going on outside. A sense of prolonged uncertainty and foreboding is growing. The feeling of peril becomes even stronger as they hear unusual sounds. *What is it?* Men are moving about. *Who are they? What do they want?* Inside the cabin, no one can see anything.

SEVENTEEN:
FOR ALL

Outside the cabin, the Frenchman is slowly bringing his rifle to the front. He holds it at the ready. With his chest pushed out and his shoulders pulled back, he smirks at his protagonist. While maintaining eye contact, he keeps his hand on the gun's trigger. Then he waits.

Now, no less than a dozen Indians encircle the cabin. Each one's armed. Some with bows and arrows, but most with Charlesville .69 caliber, standard French muskets. Could the danger possibly be any greater?

Apprehension is growing by leaps and bounds inside the cabin. Without exception, all are peering anxiously through peepholes and cracks. Bob's asking himself, *What have I gotten myself into?* Ryan's now fidgety. Earnie Smith has his arms tight against his side.

That is, that's what he does when he isn't biting his nails. Bob's rubbing the back of his neck and wringing his hands. His wide eyed pupils have dilated so much they appear much larger.

In the Choctaw's native language, Western Muskogean, Malek says, "Did you girls drop by to play stickball? I see you didn't send real warriors on this mission. All I can see is a bunch of afraid women."

Inside, near panic is running wild. Bob's asking himself, *Wonder what death feels like?*

Another inner thought crosses his mind: *Did Malek bring me here just to die?* Behind his eyes, he's flooding with salty tears. *My thinking processes are on strike.* Irrepressible tears begin streaming down his face. They're profuse but silent. He begins to plead, *Father, please intervene.*

A profound but tense silence ensues for a handful of minutes. Suddenly, Bob's shoulders pull back, and he starts grinning. In a strong and resolute voice, he asserts, "Lighten up, folks. God's still in charge. No matter what might happen, we belong to Him." With that, the mood in the room changes slightly.

EIGHTEEN:
BLOW UP

Outside, the red rim of the evening sun is getting slimmer. Without warning, Malek directs his attention to his chubby adversary. He is just now stealthily drawing back the hammer on his musket. No doubt he hopes Malek doesn't notice.

With hands on his hips, Malek raises one eyebrow and stares at porky insidiously. He projects an electrical ray from his brain to the big boy's motor Cortex (a thin strip on the top of a brain, a part of the cerebral cortex controlling the execution of voluntary and involuntary movements). He's stunned. His eyes are blinking. He stares down at his hand. It's paralyzed totally.

Malek has penetrated the man's mind. Thus, his trigger finger's frozen. Next, using his power of *electrokinesis* (psychic power to manipulate energy), Malek sets the gun afire.

All of the mechanical parts, trigger, trigger guard, hammer, frizzen, and tumbler, take on a red-hot glow. Fast as a rabbit before a prairie fire, the man drops the gun.

The gun barely hits the ground when the powder horn, suspended from his shoulder, starts turning red. He yanks the strap from over his head. He throws the horn as far as he can.

At this exact instant, BOOM! The powder horn explodes! The fiery eruption of sound and light tears through everyone, those inside and those around the cabin. The smell is smoky and sweet, like sulfur and charcoal. The heavy-set man feels like icepicks are puncturing both ears. Then, he notices all of the flesh on his left arm is missing. He screams. "Ahhhh!" His breathing becomes difficult.

The inexpressible agony in the man's obvious. Burning pain is unbearable as he falls to the ground, screaming.

A frenzy of nervous agitation sweeps through each Choctaw soldier. They're totally addled. They're bewildered as a duck flying north in the winter. All their mouths are ajar, questioning looks abound, and all of their eyes are wide. Should they run, launch a mass attack, or do something else?

Single-minded and adamant, the remaining white man is filled with invincible determination. Is he indomitable or just plain obstinate? Regardless, he decides to do what others fail at doing. His eyes narrow, and his nose wrinkles. He spits out words with contempt, "You are a dead man!" He brings his rifle up.

Suddenly, the powder horn at his side explodes. BOOM! He is no more. The smell is like no other, smokey and peppery.

Malek makes a humming noise as a thought runs through his mind. *I like using telepathy better than either of these three languages. No need to repeat anything. It goes from one mind to another. So much faster than talking.* That's what he does. His declaration goes from his mind to the minds of those encircling the cabin. He's plain, he's direct, and each Choctaw Indian, as well as any other Frenchmen in the group, knows exactly what he means. *These people serve a mighty God, unlike the sun god of you would-be warriors. If you continue to harass them, you will be destroyed.*

So what will they do? Uncertainty doesn't exist in Malek's mind. However, in the cabin, everyone's wondering, *What comes next?* "What are these savages going to do now," spoken by Earnie Smith, expresses the feelings of each one of them. Amidst feeling jittery or nervous, muscle tension, and rapid heartbeats, several possibilities come forth.

"They're gonna all start shooting at once," Earnie offers. "They be burn down our house," says Teata while shaking and trembling. Her husband offers, "At the very least, they're going to steal all of our animals."

NINETEEN:
NO BIG DEAL, ONLY A FOREST FIRE

Among the Choctaws, there's a sense of choking, shaking or trembling, and a shortness of breath. In a matter of minutes, there's clearly a consensus. Little by little, each one slowly slips away. Malek listens until they're more than a couple of miles away.

It is time to turn his attention to the raging forest fire. Right now, the out-of-control monstrous fire has become a wild inferno. It is spreading rapidly in their direction. Already, the acrid taste of smoke fills the air. Everyone inside the cabin has come outside. They stare frantically at the monstrous fire, which is devouring everything in its path. No question. That fire's rushing toward them. Dark pools of fear begin appearing under their eyes. Deep-seated nervousness is revealed in their muscle twitching and difficulty breathing. Earnie Smith puts in words what they're all thinking, "We n-n-n-need to let all the animals out and start running."

Ryan takes his suggestion seriously and starts racing toward the corral. Teata starts for the house.

In an orotund voice, loud and clear, Malek shouts, "Stop!"

"What do you mean stop?" Ryan says.

Bob also has a moment of serious doubt. His forehead puckers and his head's shaking slightly.

Malek doesn't respond. Instead, he walks slowly a few more steps away from the house.

There, he spreads his legs slightly and raises both arms. When they're even with his shoulders, he opens his palms heavenward. Everyone stares at him. What in the world is he doing? Ryan, Teata, and Earnie all look at Bob quizzically. He has no answer for them. So, what are they to do? Belatedly, Bob says, "Let's give him a minute."

Malek's eyes are closed. Nothing's happening. He just stands there with both arms extended.

Now a restless wind rustles the leaves around them. Before they can reason out their next move, the wind grows to where it rattles branches of shivering trees. Out of the blue, a savage crack of lightning creaks across the sky. The wind deepens to a roar. It continues to grow by the second. Now, it screams through the trees. It churns and boils. Malek hasn't moved an inch. With a crack of thunder, the sky is illuminated with stark blue-whiteness.

In an instant, sheets of rain are falling in torrents. With that, Malek runs and gets under the porch. With screaming and squealing, the others join him. Hard-driving rain forces them back into the cabin. Once inside, Malek confides in them, "*Verily*, the fire will be out *betimes* (within a short time)."

TWENTY:
A PERPLEXING PROBLEM

There's a huge exhalation of pent-up breath as Ryan throws his hands in the air. Without hesitation, he hugs everyone within reach. Then he looks up in a silent prayer of thanksgiving. Joyful tears are streaming down Teata's face. She smiles with her lips, her eyes, and her whole body. That smile is warm, like the first breath of spring after a cold winter or like a puppy wagging his tail. Then laughter explodes from all four of them. Even Earnie breaks out in glowing laughter.

It remains for Malek to supply a satisfying conclusion, "*Yes*, it is time to put this behind us now, and you're all safe."

It takes a while, but they all simmer down, becoming as calm as a winter night. At this point, the camaraderie grows among them even more. Bob even offers a couple of jokes, both of which he has to explain.

Ryan's full of excited energy and more than a little proud as he states, "People are going to be talking about the miraculous things that happened here.

Earnie expresses his full and complete agreement. "That's for dang shore."

Malek offers an alternate opinion, "In a few years *hither*, all of this will be seen as a legend or as folklore."

Bob's mood is exuberant, like everyone else. A few minutes earlier, he's hugging anyone within reach. In nothing flat, a sick, hollow ache blossoms inside him. In a matter of seconds, the corners of his mouth droop like a wilting flower. A pair of weighty and unwelcome thoughts have intruded into his consciousness. *What would happen were Malek and I not here? Would my ancestor have been killed?* An inescapable conclusion now stands before him. *That would then mean I would not have been born.* After a moment's contemplation, he decides to put the question to Malek. "I was just thinking, if we weren't here, what would have happened to Ryan and Teata?"

After a moment of deafening silence, Malek says, "*Howbeit*, I would have been here in any event. Ryan is also one of my assignments." As Teata puts little Delano to bed, she brings out a small, handmade flute and begins to play it. "Tootle, tootle-too, ha-dittle, how dittle." The piping is lilting and soft. Bob's impressed with the dulcet sound. For some reason, the scene reminds him once again of his Belinda, who loves to sing and is quite often humming. *I remember the first time I saw her in church. The sound of her voice floated through the air on gossamer wings. Her face was like a morning in the springtime.*

He tries not to think about the decision he will have to make. Still, it romps through his mind like the ambling gait of a wild horse. *Just thinking about it hurts.*

The next day, the sun is drifting softly toward the western flat lands as Bob and Malek make their way back eastward toward one of only five gaps through the Appalachians. A gentle breeze rippling through the trees is invigorating. An assortment of wondrous earthy smells waft through their nostrils.

Bob raises a question suggesting he has been deep in thought, "If Ryan had been killed back there, does that mean I would never have been born?"

Malek doesn't even turn aside. Instead, he says, "*For sooth*, it would alter history in some respects. *Howbeit*, this is probably not the best time to discuss eternalism and the Grandfather Paradox."

Not satisfied with his answer, Bob enquires, "What about Ryan's family, how do they do in the future?"

Malek explains, "In a few years, that chubby little boy, Delano, will have two sons. The older of them, Winston, will have two sons and three daughters. Winston *sore* likes to fight. I'm not talking about brawling *nowise*; I mean, it's a sport for him. He and a friend of his set up these boxing matches all over. *Aye*, I really enjoy watching him box. *Nowise*, did he ever lose a fight." With that, he pauses and rolls his eyes. Then he continues, "He joins men from Virginia and the Senecas to fight with Major George Washington and defeat the French. *Howbeit*, he will be killed in that 1754 event."

"*Tother* son, the younger one, Fletcher, will raise and train horses on what will become the family farm.

TWENTY-ONE: HUNDRED YEAR JUMP

Bob's getting winded as the two of them trudge uphill on this mountain road. The rocky lane is seldom traveled, and the multitude of scattered rocks and disagreeable brush don't make their journey any easier. A breeze is rippling through leaves on the ground. The quick movements of a scampering antelope a few feet away, draws Bob's attention.

That instant, Malek announces, "*Erelong* we are about to make another trip?"

Bob's response is, "Another hundred years into the past, or in the future?"

Uncharacteristically, Malek makes a humming noise and answers immediately. "*Methinks* you have no idea how important the number one hundred is? *Yea,* it's mentioned fifty-five times in the Bible. *Forsooth*, Noah, Sarah, and Moses lived to be a hundred…"

Bob interrupts him with, "Can we get started?"

Malek stares at him without saying a word. Finally, he pronounces, "We are going to time travel from *hither tother* hundred years this time."

Blinking his eyes, Bob responds, "AYS (are you serious)? We're not going home?"

Malek looks at him indifferently, saying, "We are talking about chronokinesis or time manipulation." Bob can see movement in Malek's temple. From the biology class he teaches, he remembers the spot is also known as the *pterion*, the place where four skull bones fuse together. An ill-defined and scary idea about what this means saunters through his head unbidden.

Malek points out, "Place-shifting and time-shifting cannot be done together. Let's shift places *afore tother*. You ready?" With that, Malek takes his hand. Bob shivers. The sensation surges first in his hands. The feeling is neither pleasing nor painful. Quickly, it moves up his arms and his legs. Then, it progresses to his chest and shoulders, where it's stronger. Straight away, it rushes through his head and face. His surroundings become hazy with no discernable shapes. He shivers. Colors are rapidly shifting. Hundreds of unrecognizable images flash before him.

When the environment settles down, Bob cannot recognize anything. He finds himself on a dusty road, deep in a forest. Pine trees are extremely dense. The aromatic scent is sharp, sweet, and invigorating. A breeze is rippling through the trees.

"So, we're in 1824," Malek announces without emotion.

Bob responds with, "Hmm, 1824, the year Congress establishes Arkansas Territory and Mexico becomes a republic."

Malek offers no reply. As the two of them shuffle down the road, a variety of sounds become clearer. There's music, rowdy and noisy, throbbing and undulating. There's the sound of people yelling and howling. The recognizable sound of a speaker is piercing, continuous, and loud. Then, there's the sound of squealing along with several unrecognizable sounds.

Various unidentifiable aromas are now drifting through the air and hits him in the face. The pungent odor of wood burning stirs him and reminds him of the camping trip he and Belinda went on together. *Making s'mores over the fire, after walking the trails….* The rich, almost toxic smell of a multitude of campfires tends to tickle their noses. *One smells good, thousands at one time, not so much.* The earthy odor of thousands of animals, even this far away, makes their eyes burn. On top of that, the rank body odor of thousands of human beings is also becoming a bit disagreeable.

Straight away, ahead of them, is some kind of opening. As they get closer, Bob recognizes it as a group of corrals or enclosures of some kind. Walking past them, Bob wonders, *How many horses and mules are here?*

As though he has been reading Bob's mind, Malek replies, "Must be hundreds of mules and oxen, besides."

Tumultuous crowd noises are becoming louder, gibbering, hooting, roaring, yelping, and chattering. That noise grows more rude and riotous as they get closer. With the multitude of animals behind them, they come upon a city. It's a city of tents, wagons, draped in coverings and open-air camps. They're set up concentrically, swirling around a brush-covered arbor. Dozens of elevated tripods, where at night fire will be for lights, are scattered about throughout. Men and women are moving purposefully among them. *There's an awful lot of coming and going.*

Cooking fires are being attended to; children not so much. The children are scurrying about, laughing and yelling. A few are running about like wild animals.

In amazement, Bob declares, "Thousands and thousands of people must live here."

Malek replies, "Yeah, *verily,* at least for four or five days."

Looking around, Bob enquires, "Where are we, anyway?"

Malek responds, "We are at the Coon Creek Camp Meeting here in north central Tennessee."

Bob's astonished at all he sees. He's at a loss for words. Bubbly and upbeat, finally, he says, "Let's check this out." Together, they stroll through the brush arbor. It all renders him dumb-founded, except for an occasional "Omagosh."

TWENTY-TWO: IS THAT PREACHING?

At the center of everything, in the brush-covered shelter, people are sitting on split log benches. Some are laughing, and others are raising their hands and yelling. At the front is a mourner's bench, already with two men down on their knees. In front of that is a rudely constructed preaching platform. The man currently exhorting the crowd is extremely loud and animated. He's wearing a long tailcoat, cut away in front, with a tall standing collar.

He doesn't have a beard, but he does have graying mutton chops. Eight other preachers sit on the platform. Malek answers the unspoken question, "Yes, they are all waiting *erlong* for their turn. The one preaching is a Baptist farmer. *Tothers* are Presbyterian drum pounders or Methodist circuit-riders, and *tother* kinds..."

Bob stops to listen. *That preacher doesn't have very good grammar.*

"You muffin-walloper, you scandal-loving blowsabellas, judgement be coming fer y'all. I'm afeared God's patience be done run out. You guys be shinning around, corned wid squeezins. Me, I be betwattled He let you live this long."

His face's red. Spittle's on his lip. His voice's thunderous, resounding through the camp.

Listeners respond differently. "Amen!" is heard from four corners. "Hallelujahs!" also pierces the air, pulsating from ear to ear. In the aisle running beside Bob, a man falls to the ground as though he were dead. Within a few minutes, he's back up on his feet. Some of the folks are raising their hands and waving. Others are rolling their eyes.

Three rows behind Bob, a woman wearing a bonnet, like most women here, starts barking like a dog, "Wolf, wolf!" She takes a breath and starts again. "Wolf! Wolf!" Bob shakes his head, with his eyebrows drawn together in a tight downward arch.

TWENTY-THREE: PRAYING, PARTIES AND A WHOOPERUP

All of the rumbling in this strange situation is more than a bit unnerving. However, what happens next is even more disconcerting. In front of Bob, on the next split log, a man goes into involuntary convulsions. His head jerks forward and backward violently. At the same time, a woman on the pew behind him hysterically laughs out loud. "Ha, ha!" Bob's puzzled. What's so *funny?*

Malek offers, "Emotional ecstasy is what they call it."

Bob picks up on that, "If indeed it can be rightly called that, it is spreading through the crowd. *Perhaps,* ...Bob reasons, *maybe it's some kind of mass hysteria. Whatever it is, it comes on rapidly and leaves the same way.*

Even so, Bob isn't ready for what happens next. The young man, now standing next to him, is weeping uncontrollably. *What should I do? How can I help him?* Before he can resolve his dilemma, the young man throws his arms around him. He's trim and muscular.

His dark hair is long. He has dark, nut-brown eyes and trimmed eyebrows. He also has a beard, a mustache, and a mole under his right eye.

"Please," he whimpers. "Don't turn away like I did. Let Jesus in." He's bawling his eyes out and desperately sucking in breaths between sobs. "He has made such a wonderful difference in my life." The young man grips Bob and holds him even more tightly.

Gently, Bob pushes him back and says, "Wait. Jesus already lives in my heart."

In a shaky voice, he says, "Wow! That's fantastic!" He's silent for just a moment and then says, "I'm Leroy Mitchell. Would you like to have dinner with me and my family. My maw's a hard-down good cook."

Bob responds, "I'm Bob Becker, and this is Malek." With a nod of Malek's head, they agree to accept the dinner invitation.

Leroy suggests, "Let's go eat right now. I'm hungry enough to eat the handle off a hoe."

Bob responds, "Shouldn't we wait 'till the service is over?"

Leroy answers, "These services go on all day long and way into the night. Jevver sit in church that long?"

As they tramp through various makeshift camps, around tents and wagons, as well as scores of adults and children. Bob finds it hard to believe what his eyes behold. By contrast, Malek looks as if the whole thing is commonplace. Each camp has a limited space around a wagon, a tent, or a makeshift lean-to. Making their way to his family's camp amounts to working through a maze. "Avoid that fire. Watch out for that child. Uh-oh, sorry." The noise is pulsating. The chattering, the jabbering, and the sobbing are rowdy. As they walk, Leroy explains, "These folks are poor as Job's turkey."

Here and there, Bob can't help noticing several small groups, with all of them down on their knees, obviously praying. Some of these meetings are operating in total silence. Bob endeavors to move softly around them. Other groups are resounding with three or four folks praying aloud at once, uproariously loud and noisy. Bob chews it over, *Remarkable*. His face is a picture of incredulity.

A few steps later, they encounter more gatherings, which actually amount to full-blown preaching services. They pause for a moment outside of one of these. An older man is haranguing a small group.

"I'm afeared some of you bad eggs be headed straight to hell. Ponder whar you be going. Don't be vazey (stupid). You may have a fimble-famble (lame excuse), but thar ain't none. Can it be in this here boodle (crowd)…"

Leroy's opinion of this speaker is, "He don't know spit from noodles." Woven in between and around his words are the sounds of music drifting in from other areas. Bob can identify the sound of banjos, "Twang plunk plink." He also recognizes a fiddle, "Fiddle-fiddle dee."

The music is clamorous while being a bit sparkling and giddy. On top of that, nearby someone's singing. Distantly, others are singing, but only one is recognizable from where they are. Leroy calls her a, "Whooperup (a second rate singer)." Perhaps, but her words can be heard near and far, "Conceive yourself quite lucky. For 'tis not often that you see a hunter from Kentucky."

A party's definitely going on over there. As they get closer, Bob sees several people dancing and celebrating. Dust and leaves are being kicked up. A few are what Leroy calls a shincrackers," or good dancers. Most are simply cavorting about, expressing their incredibly laid back, feel-good feelings. Now he can see a harmonica helping provide music. Bob listens to the "wah wah" of a hand vibrato. All of it certainly is lively and exhilarating, a goodtime frolic. The gladness must be contagious because they pass at least a half dozen other such blowouts before reaching their destination. Sticky bodies are whirling, stomping in the dust and stumbling. Laughter is boisterous, deep-throated, and knee-slapping. Clearly, at least for a time, those who toil and struggle are suffused with obvious joy. At this point, Malek explains to Bob, "*Alas*, this is one of the few social activities here on the frontier."

A man comes running toward them, working up a sweat. Bob's a bit apprehensive. *He may be running from someone or after someone.* But the fellow scurries past them at full tilt. "What's up with him?" Bob asks of Leroy.

Leroy giggles and explains, "I allow as how it's a religious exercise. Bleeve me, it happens a plenty in these meetin's. He'll run throo the woods 'till he wears himself out. Then he's bawlin' and squawlin'. Exhausted, he'll feel closer to God, or least that's how they tawlk. I'm thinkin' their lid ain't on too tight. When you see a boy and a young lady slippin' out into the woods, like 'em over thar, …she ain't wearin' 'nuff to pad a crutch…they've got somethin' else on their minds."

Most of the people they encounter are cordial and friendly. A few are not so much so.

Coon Creek Camp Meeting

Most of the women wear dresses of wool or flax, fabric they themselves have planted, harvested, and processed. Fabrics imported, including calico, flannel, and Irish linen, are expensive. Thus, very few dresses made of these materials are here. Most wear aprons, tied at the waist or pinafore style. Almost all women are wearing bonnets with a lightweight cap underneath and alone indoors. Still, Leroy refers to several as, "Eye-ball pleasers."

Men wear pullover linen or wool shirts with long, full sleeves. Many wear a hunting shirt, made of deer skin and fur with scads of fringe. Suspenders are everywhere, but no belts. Leather boots, with tops turned down, have flat souls. There is also a super-abundance of wide-brim felt hats. Another thing in abundance here is beards.

TWENTY-FOUR: TOM MITCHELL FAMILY

The Mitchells turn out to be a hard-working farm family, who are ever so proud of their son, who actually works in a bank. His mother proudly explains, "He purt-near educated himself. He's hard down good at doing sums."

Leroy jumps in with, "I educated mysef wid ma's help."

His mother, is a petite lady, like a pyramid orchard. She has lovely open lips with slightly gray teeth behind them. Her hair is bundled at the neck behind her. Her voice is captivating, bubbling with enthusiasm. Bob has no trouble imagining how nice having a birth mother like her would be. Kicking that idea around, he concludes *Belinda would be that kind of mother. Wonder how many children we would have? What would they be like?*

Tom Mitchell, Leroy's father, is lean and muscular, especially for a fifty-year-old. He has angular nostrils in a bony nose. There's real character in his mud–brown eyes, though nets of wrinkles are at the corners. Authority is in his deep voice. Though at times, it creaks like a rusty gate.

Turns out Leroy has two teenage sisters. Both of them are immediately intrigued by Bob. Jenny, the older of the two, compliments him at every opportunity. Carol flips her hair flirtatiously when she thinks he's watching.

Bob doesn't pick up on what's happening—at least at first. Malek's amused by their behavior. Both of them listen intently to what he says, with different smiles. They touch him at every opportunity. Bob soon decides the Mitchells, Jill, and Pete, as they insist their guests call them, are warm and accepting. Neither of them asks any obtrusive questions. By contrast, Carol is extremely inquisitive of Bob, "Where are you from? Do you have any immediate plans, and do you have a family at home?" Malek does a good job deflecting her questions without being rude.

Jenny's more direct, "Do you have sum one in mind for a wife?"

TWENTY-FIVE: GREAT CORNBREAD

With a nervous smile, Bob answers, "That's yet to be decided." For his part, Malek looks as if his face has misplaced its smile. The question's disturbing for Bob.

As the ladies continue preparing dinner, the men discuss how the camp meeting is going. Pete allows, "As how thar has to be over ten thousand folks here, from all around."

Jenny tries to maintain soft eye contact with Bob, as she says, "I have trouble singing along with some of the songs."

Leroy shares, "For us, Camp Meetin' is always a vacation."

His Dad jumps in, saying, "We only come to meeting after our crops are laid by."

Leroy adds, "And it was a great place to meet girls."

Before he can go farther, Jenny laughingly says, "You only look at her gams (legs)." She covers her mouth, giggling.

Her sister, Carol, quickly corrects, "No, he looks at her cat-heads (breasts)."

Leroy rebukes, "Shut your pan."

Deliberately, Bob changes the subject, "If my observations are any indication, there's a lot of he-ing and she-ing going on around here."

Leroy continues, "But this year has been altogether different. Three nights ago, I had an experience that changed me and my life completely. I had a personal encounter with my Lord. And I can't wait to tell Katy."

Malek poses a one-word question, "Katy?"

Before Leroy can answer, his Dad explains, "Katy Morningside, is the daughter of the bank's president, whar Leroy wuks." There's an undercurrent of disdain in his voice.

Leroy goes on to explain, "She's the girl I love and plan to marry up wif." As the words come from him, his father rolls his eyes.

At that moment, Jill announces, "Dinner's ready." Then, looking at Bob, she says, "You two, put your nose in the manger." Bob looks perplexed with a dimwitted look on his face, so she explains, "You two have a seat on these here stools, and we'll eat perpendicular."

Turns out, dinner features roast chicken. Two whole birds, cooked over the campfire, are juicy and flavorful. Bob finds it to be succulent. Malek especially enjoys the leafy mustard-greens, with a strong mustard taste. He calls them "greens with attitude." Everyone enjoys the hot, buttery cornbread, with the dominant ingredient of corn. The all-around favorite is dessert, an out-of-this-world blackberry pudding. Both Bob and Malek have seconds.

While they're eating, Leroy tells everyone about Katy, though his family has heard it all before. "She has long, purt-near perfect, blond hair. And, them blue eyes are hard down good lookin'. She has beautiful pink lips like purple clover. Whunsinawhal (Once in a while) I look at her feminine curves. They are real eyeball pleasers. Bleeve me, I allow as how her lags be long and shapely."

Both of Leroy's sisters are giggling for all they're worth. His father inserts, "Scuse me, besides all of this tomfoolery, how much do you really know 'bout this young lady? What beliefs does she have? When it comes to the lady's body parts, my giveadammer's broken. Stead-uf her shape, you need ta find out 'bout her relationship wid the Lord." Looking at Bob and then at Malek, he adds, "When it comes to her Dad, J. Gilbert Morningside, he thinks he's the only berry on the bush."

TWENTY-SIX:
KATY, KATY

With Malek's supernatural ability, three days later amounts to only a couple minutes for the two time-travelers. The thought creeps into Bob's mind unbidden. *Is all of this a series of wondrous dreams? Will I awaken and discover none of this is real? Is Malek only a hallucination or a delusion?*

Sitting on a porch in a small North Tennessee town, Bob's in a good mood as he recalls all the things he learned at the camp meeting. He has decided which one of the preachers he likes best and which one of Jill Mitchell's meals he enjoyed the most. Thinking about the Mitchell's two daughters, he ponders again, *Should I ask Belinda to marry me? Am I going to live long enough to be married? She would have the burden of taking care of an invalid. We would have a short life together. How would I ever be able to give her all the things I promised her?*

Here, on a mammoth hill at the confluence of the Cumberland and the Red Rivers, a sizable town, has developed. Indeed, it has become, in a short time, a center of commerce.

Dark-fired tobacco has become a sensation and is greatly sought after in Europe. For the last four years, steamboats left port here for New Orleans or Pittsburg, full of this tobacco. To a lesser degree, they also export cotton, flour, and corn. Railroads are yet a few years away and flatboats are rapidly disappearing. For the time being, Clarksville is the trafficking center of middle Tennessee. Bob and Malek have walked about the city, especially noting the Custom House, where tobacco is inspected, and the newly built First Presbyterian Church. To say that Bob remains unimpressed is understatement. However, were he is as knowledgeable and as aware as Malek, he would know Leroy is even now telling his beautiful Katy all about his experience at the camp meeting. He finds her at home alone.

He's enraptured as he tells her about all the different sermons he heard. He's euphoric recounting the various spiritual expressions he has witnessed. He's on the edge of his seat, trying to explain all that has happened to him. Katy's eyelids are drooping. Her legs are crossed, and one foot's shaking. She has an uneven smile as she grips her upper arms. "My life's completely changed," he tells her. "Since I let Jesus into my heart, I'm an altogether different man."

He's delirious and throbbing with excitement as he waits for her response.

Rolling her eyes with an uneven smile, she comments, "That doesn't really matter."

He swallows hard and shakes his head as he winches with a pained expression. He waits a moment, and then, with words soft as rain, he pronounces, "I'm madly in love wif you an' I want you to have what I have." He again stares into her clear blue eyes. They're dancing eyes glistening. Staring into those sparkling eyes, love-struck Leroy pleads, "Will you be my wife?"

TWENTY-SEVEN: IN THE JAILHOUSE NOW

The next morning, Malek awakens Bob with a gentle nudge. "You better get up *anon*; it isn't good." Hurriedly, Bob gets dressed. *Oh how I hate putting on these hose and I despise these shoes.* Afterward, the two of them rush into the street, where they hurry down first one street and then another. Bob's quizzical of his mentor, but no answers are forthcoming, even though his lips are parted, and his eyebrows are raised in inquiry. As they reach the end of the block, Bob's shocked at what Malek tells him.

"Leroy is under arrest," Malek explains. "Now he is being locked in the Montgomery County Jail."

Doesn't take long for the two of them to get there, and they arrive just as the cell door clangs on him. Bob shutters as Leroy yells, "What did I do? Somebody tell me what I did."

The officer, a mean and burly bull calf, snarls at him, "You'll find out soon enough." Then he shoves him forward. Turning his attention to Malek and Bob, he growls, "You two get said whatever you 'ave to say and get out uf here."

Leroy's fighting back the tears as he nervously tramps back and forth inside the small cell. "What's happenin' to me," he laments, shaking his head. With strong feelings jumbled together, he's trembling and shaking. His surroundings exacerbate the situation. Aside from being meager, the cell's demon-dirty and tedious gray. It's also putrid beyond words. Musty and rank.

Bob looks at Malek, hoping for an answer. His heart's beating faster as he stares unwaveringly. *I wonder, how does he feel? Maybe he feels like he has cancer in his soul. I can relate.*

Malek waits a moment. He watches Leroy, but his face does not reveal the empathy he feels for both young men. In a slow but deliberate voice, he says, "Leroy, you have been accused of embezzling money from the bank where you work."

"No! That can't be!" Leroy declares. "How do you know that?"

Bob answers for his friend, "Oh, he just knows stuff."

A swell of rage rises in Leroy's face and soon nearly consumes him. Bob tries to calm him down, reminding him, "All things work together for good them that love the Lord."

The atmosphere slowly improves as Bob offers encouragement. Looking around, he counts three other cells in the room, but the others are empty. Bob begins running the situation through his mind, looking for answers. *This man's my ancestor, at least that's what Malek tells me. That being the case, I should help him. But how? If he really is a criminal, does it make a difference?* He looks over at Malek, standing beside him. As usual, he's stony-faced, totally unimpassioned. That's when Katy walks in.

TWENTY-EIGHT: INSULT TO INJURY

Seeing Katy, Leroy lights up, smacking his lips. "I'm so glad you came to this awful place to see me. Dear, sweet Katy," he says. "I'm sure you know I didn't do what they say I did."

Bob looks at Malek, seeking advice on whether they should leave the two of them alone.

Malek doesn't respond. In fact, he doesn't move a muscle.

Soon after arriving, Katy bursts into tears. Her shoulders tremble as she blubbers. "Sob sob, waah." Wiping back the wet, she says haltingly, "I came to tell you I can't marry you."

Leroy looks as though he has been hit in the face. Shaking his head back and forth and rubbing his arms absently, Leroy's at a loss for words. Finally, raising his hands in the air, he says, "No, you can't. You told me last night you would marry me. We can work through this." Her only response is shaking her head.

He's rocking back and forth and breathing heavier. Wet spots are appearing below his eyes. Next, he turns away, covering his mouth. Sounding slightly hollow, she says, "I know I said last night I would, but I just can't." At this point, she stops and wipes her face with a handkerchief. "I told my Daddy how excited you were by all the stuff that happened at the camp meeting. He said all of that was good. Then I told him you proposed to me and then he took on a weird look. I asked him what was the matter, but he said it was nothing. This morning, when I went by the bank, he told me $1,000 was missing. He said you took it. I told him you wouldn't do such a thing. He said, 'Nobody else could have done it.'"

With quivering lips and stinging tears streaming down his face, Leroy mournfully says, "I didn't take any money. Your father's wrong. He made a mistake."

TWENTY-NINE: CONFRONTING A BANKER

After Katy leaves, the two of them hang around as long as the guard allows. Walking back down the street, Bob's admiring the wildflowers, especially the Blue Veruvain. He asks, "So what do we do now?"

True to his normal comportment, Malek appears as though he could care less. Pointing toward the river, he calls Bob's attention to two smokestacks on top of a steamboat, two dark and towering, a silhouette against the morning sun. "*Behold*, those boats are taking over all the river traffic."

Bob enquires, "Is that where we're going?" Malek says nothing. Another block, and he points at the Riverside Bank. Walking into the bank lobby, Bob isn't sure why they're here.

J. Gilbert Morningside's a big guy. One would be tempted to call him a lardass. He's bald-headed, a real baldilocks, and wears glasses halfway down his nose. He wears a black, three-piece suit with a cut-away coat and stiff collar. He walks with a swagger, hands stuffed in his pockets.

In Morningside's office, Malek produces a few gold nuggets and says, "Before getting involved with your bank," he asserts, "we have some concerns about the bank's dealing with a friend of ours, Leroy Mitchell. Can you help us understand what's happening with him?"

Morningside turns his head as he says, "I think I heard something about that. One of the other employees was talking about it."

More than a little irritated, Bob says, "But, we heard that you. .."

Talking over him, Morningside demands. "Do you know who I am?" Aggravation is growing in his voice as he declares, "I built this bank to where it is, all by myself. I am the most respected man in this city." His words spew with contempt.

Malek stands to his feet and gestures with both hands, "We didn't come *hither* to upset you; howbeit, we simply want to find out what happened to our friend."

In a bellicose tone, the banker responds, "Well, the best thing I can tell you is you need to get a better quality of friends. This nitwit crony of yours is uneducated, indolent, and totally lacking in any redeeming virtues."

Malek turns toward the door, signaling Bob to do the same. Their exit is fast and deliberate.

Out on the street, several steps away from the bank, Malek poses a question for his young friend. "*Prithee,* what did you learn from that collogue (private talk)?"

Bob quickly responds, "First thing I learned is that man hates Leroy."

Malek replies, "*Maybe* that *scurvy* fellow *doth* not hate him, *howbeit* he certainly *doth* not want him marrying his daughter *nowise. Verily,* we also learned from that *brabbe* (loud, dumb argument) that he is a liar, and he lied about your ancestor."

THIRTY: JAILBREAK ANYONE?

Bob does a little eye-rubbing as he leans in toward Malek. In a softened tone of voice, he asks, "How did we get that?"

They stop for a moment, as Malek explains, "He *hath* no eye contact and no contractions. His answers *doth* imply rather than answering the question. *Howbeit*, he added all those unnecessary details."

Immersed in thought with a contemplative expression, Bob joins Malek in walking again. A few steps later, he pauses again and asks, somewhat facetiously, "What difference does it make if that wisenheimer is a liar?"

They have gone a full two blocks before Malek answers him. "*Ere* we break your in-law out of jail. Hence, we will be breaking the law." That gets Bob's attention instantly. After a moment and a few more steps, he continues, "Howbeit, I wanted you to know verily that Leroy's innocent. *Forsooth,* he was jailed falsely."

Bob's jubilant as they enter the jail. Once again the fatty-patty jailer is sitting at a beat-up old desk, drowsy and nodding. As the two of them enter, he waves half-heartedly and yawns. Walking past him, Malek places a light hand on the jailor's shoulder. Immediately, his head droops, and he begins snoring. Leroy's surprised to see them. His eyebrows are high and curved as his lower jaw drops. Without saying a word, Malek puts his hand on the cell door's lock. A gentle touch unlocks it.

A huge exhalation of pent-up breath flies from Leroy. "How did you do that," he asks, as he grabs his hat and hurriedly walks out of the cell. After throwing both of his hands in the air, he hugs them. When he regains his composure, he insists they tell him, "Am I really free?"

Bob and Malek hurry him out of the city. Within a short space of time, they're outside of town. Malek gently takes him by the arm and explains, "*Forsooth*, you have to find a new dwelling place, not just someplace, *mayhap* you need to move farther west, thither, out on the frontier."

He agrees with them. But he's unsure of one thing, "What about Katy? I love her."

Bob listens to Leroy, really listens. The easy part is hearing how profoundly Leroy loves Katy. He feels life will be empty without her, and wonders if he can live without her. *I can feel what Leroy's feeling.* He thinks of his own fiancé. *Know how I would feel if I were never to see Belinda again.* With an empathetic tone and a hand on his shoulder, he says, "I can see you're really upset. It must be really difficult for you. Still, you have to realize she doesn't love you. You have to move on."

Tears flood his eyes. Wrapping an arm around him, Malek repeats what Bob has said, saying, "You must admit she didn't really love you."

In that instant, a catastrophic menace appears below the horizon, behind them.

THIRTY-ONE: POSSE ANYONE?

At first, Bob isn't sure what it is. His seeing a dust cloud is obvious. The question is what or who's causing it. Thinking it through, Bob concludes *Several people are coming this way and they're coming fast.*

Pointing at the thick and frightful cloud, he asks, "Who is that?" *I know he knows who they are and what they want.* Though he tries to conceal it, his apprehension is obvious.

Malek explains, "*Forsooth*, the county sheriff, and a hurriedly assembled possere coming after me, you, and Leroy. *Howbeit*, they are motivated by that *scurvy* banker."

Bob's adrenaline spikes; he starts feeling jittery or nervous. *My skin's crawling*, he admits to himself. He starts gasping and expelling his breath. It isn't mind-bending dread yet, but it's on its way.

Leroy freezes in place. But, with a false bravado, he tries to pretend he isn't scared.

Even so, his breathing becomes rapid. Images of what could be, flashes in his mind. His breath catches in his throat.

Malek gives both of them an empathic look. Imperturbable, he says nothing. He's breathing normally and standing proud. In fact, he's calm as a summer breeze. When he does speak, it's to Leroy. "*Anon*, you need to go *whithersoever*, as quickly as you can. *Verily*, it's *meet* for Bob and I to stay here and turn this misguided posse around."

Within a matter of minutes, Leroy's out of sight, and the posse is clearly visible. It's moving at a gallop. The dust cloud its raising is becoming more ominous. Bob wants to run, though he knows he can't outrun horses. His sense of foreboding is growing. He's wondering, *What will happen to me if they catch us?*

That's when it happens.

THIRTY-TWO:
WIND-BLOWN GRIME TO THE RESCUE

With no warning and no prologue, a wall of dust and debris suddenly appears. The wall of brown air isn't smoke. Nor is it a stratus cloud. And it isn't drifting lazily across the sky either. It's an immense cloud of especially thick powder, what's called "haboob" in Arabic. It's thick and blinding. It is also dry and bitter.

Bob's shaking his head. A heavy feeling is in his stomach. "How could this happen?"

The dry and bitter grime is now getting precariously close. It's wind-driven and churning.

It screams through the trees, coming from all directions at once. It's burning their eyes.

They have to close them. It sandblasts their skin. Bob pulls his shirt up to cover his mouth and eyes.

At this point, Malek asserts, "It's worse on those fellows and their horses. *Erlong*, they'll be turning back." He's quiet for a moment and then says, "*Mayhaps* we should get on our way as well."

Leaving the blinding sand behind them, the two of them walk along, making their way west. Finding a resting place after a while, Bob admits, "I'm really glad I got to meet Leroy and get to know him. He's remarkable." Then, he remains quiet for a few minutes. His mind rambles around from one topic to another. At length, he casually mentions, "Wish we could see more than a snapshot, you know, see how things work out for Leroy."

Malek's answer is a rigid, unmoving posture, an unblinking stare into the unabashed clear blue sky. They do not stay around and wait. Instead, they join hands and make another leap through space. They also skip ahead some seven years to April, 1832. Once there, Bob's rooted to the spot. With widened eyes, he scans the area all around him. Horizontal wrinkles quickly form on his forehead.

THIRTY-THREE: ST LOUIS, REALLY?

A shabby little river town is around Bob. It appears to be full of hovels, dilapidated wooden fences, and stray dogs. He winches, with a pained expression on his face. He demands, "Where are we?"

Malek rolls his eyes, then says, "This is St. Louis, my boy; can't you see all of those steamboats on the river? It has not yet become the great westward launching point it will become."

When reality sets in, shoving disbelief aside, Bob looks at Malek and comes out with, "Tell me how you did that."

With his jaw thrust forward and his face imperturbable, Malek looks out across the Mississippi River. After a long pause, he says, "*Peradventure*, if you had the equivalent of three Ph.D. degrees combined, you might comprehend the basics of Trans-sphere mathematics. Verily, then I might be able to explain time-space modifications to you."

As they walk along the river's edge, Bob's fascinated with a dozen or so steamboats docked here. Seeing the real thing creates a great deal more awe than simply looking at pictures. *They're so large and so shimmering.* Even when docked, these boats are well-lighted. That is, aside from those exceedingly tall smokestacks. They're blackened from the smoke.

Both of them are quiet for a few minutes. Then, out of the blue, Bob asks, "How far is it from here to Memphis?"

Malek's caught off guard by the question and offers no comment other than the simple answer, "Two hundred eighty-five miles."

He fondly recalls that day he and Belinda strolled along, in a park, beside this same river. The thought runs through his mind: *Love comes down to being a constant aching. Balmy air breezed through my nostrils. The sky's hue was slowly darkening, and the world was bathed in a warm glow, the way it is this evening. Oh, how I miss her. I asked her to tell me all the things she liked about me.* He smiles as his mind joyfully runs down the list she gave him.

At the bottom of the list, he returns his mind to the present. The evening sky is reflected in the calm water of the Mississippi.

His attention is drawn to the pulsating sound of a calliope. The rapid, staccato rhythm can't be ignored. Turning his attention back toward the river, Bob fixes his gaze on yet another sternwheeler arriving from New Orleans. It's clearly the source of the music. Only a few yards away from shore now, he can read the ship's name, "Glencoe." It will dock here at the foot of Chestnut Street.

The flat bottom ship has a shallow draft of four feet. Below deck is full of over two hundred tons of cargo, animals for the most part. Boilers are on the main deck. Ordinary or regular passengers are also crowded on this deck. In New Orleans, they paid $5 for a ticket. They were also required to furnish their own meals. When the ship encounters a snag or some other obstacle to the ship's progress, they are forced to disembark and remove the impasse.

Sixty-four passengers occupy the upper deck, many of whom are out of their rooms, leaning against or over the railing. They're joyful that their journey is almost over. Ladies are wearing long skirts and bonnets. Men are dressed in cut-away coats and top hats.

Everyone's talking, laughing and waving. Above them is the Hurricane Deck, used by the captain easily recognized by his cap and beard.

BWOOM!

THIRTY-FOUR: RIVERBOAT DISASTER

Suddenly, there's a massive explosion. Spears of fire erupt through every door, window, and crack of the ship. They're shooting in every direction. The sound's deafening. The very ground trembles. It's so loud, that Bob feels like icepicks plunge in both ears. *It feels like I was punched hard in the back of the head.* The shock wave throws Bob to the rough wooden wharf, filled with cracks and splinters. As he slams into ground, he catches a glimpse of the entire pilothouse flying through the air. He's disoriented for a few minutes. Then, he's hit with a giant flood of sensations. *What was it?*

Dozens of passengers are thrown into the water. Several more are thrown onto the wharf and into the building that borders it. Others are repelled into nearby ships.

Malek rushes to help Bob to his feet. He's trembling.

Malek explains it, "All three boilers exploded."

Bob responds, "It felt like an earthquake." While he can't define or explain it: Bob experiences Barotrauma, damage to his hearing.

Most of the passengers on the main deck are killed instantly. Several passengers from the upper deck are thrown into the water. The captain's Pilot House is blown away from the ship, with the captain inside.

In parts of the ship, not decimated, several people jump from the boat in panic. Others are unable to escape their room. People are hurt and bleeding on the ship, on the dock, and in the water. Dozens more run and feverishly scurry about, looking for a way to escape.

The explosion is heard over the entire city. A roaring fire engulfs the ship. It also produces fires on three other ships and two warehouses beside the wharf. The Glenco is slowly drifting out into the middle of the river. There, it will burn down to the waterline and then sink.

After the heatwave comes a disturbing calm; dozens of passengers are still in the water. Without numbers, people are severely wounded and unable to move on their own.

They're burnt. They're bleeding. They're moaning and groaning.

Amidst all the chaos, Malek says, "Get it together, Bob. We need to help get these people out of here." Both of them immediately start identifying those still living and those already gone. While several men are struggling to pull people from the water, Bob and Malek concentrate on those on the waterfront landing.

The Glenco Explodes

THIRTY-FIVE:
OLD FRIEND, NEW FRIEND

Bob draws Malek's attention to the two steamboats on either side of the Glenco. They, too, are now burning out of control. A sea of angry flames, blazing, white-hot, are streaking upward.

Out of the blue, here comes Leroy, jumping down from a wagon. Bob's wonderstruck. A gasp of surprise and a slight smile slip from him. Leroy waves and goes to work. Without greetings, salutation, or even "Hello," they both run and jump on one of the two other ships.

Frantically, they go from room to room, helping people escape. They move burning timbers, free passengers, and struggle through debris.

At the same time, Malek prevents a ship that had been on the other side of the Glenco from blowing up. He does that by knowing where the valve on the high-pressure steam engine is found and by turning it off. He then leads out a dozen people, through smoke, to the shore.

Another horse-drawn wagon arrives on the scene. The driver's shouting, "Bring the wounded here!" The disaster scene is becoming more and more serious. Towering columns of flame are upward from riverside buildings. The fire's spreading from one building to another in the blink of an eye. Dark smoke is everywhere. Twisted metal debris and splintered wood are causing barriers. They're scattered all over and have to be overcome to reach those wounded and bleeding. Bob's moving carefully and struggling arduously. Here and there, he hears cries for help. In addition to assisting those who are injured, they try to encourage all the victims. Joined and helped by several other men, they are in a race against time. Screams can still be recognized in the wind.

Later, back on the dock, the three of them pull five people out of the water. Several other men have now arrived to help extricate those remaining in the water or onboard a ship.

Within minutes, that number of would-be rescuers grows into the hundreds. The three join right in, assisting others. They load the wounded into wagons and carts. They're rushed to hospitals.

THIRTY-SIX: RESCUE TURNS TO MURDER

A hundred yards from the wharf, a man's struggling in the water. He's waving his arms and yelling, "Help! Help!" Bob drops what he's doing and heads toward the drowning man.

Two men, closer than Bob, jump in the water. Malek and Bob, insatiably engaged, watch the rescue. As the two men get closer to the man in peril, events take a different turn. Even from where they are, Bob and Malek can see the drowning man is black.

Neither one of them is prepared for what happens next. The two would-be rescuers hold the black man under the water. He thrashes about frantically.

As loud as he can, Bob yells, "Don't!"

Even louder, Malek yells, "Stop!"

Then, unbelievably, the man's body goes limp. He's floating face down. The body begins drifting downstream.

Bob gawks in disbelief. The blood drains from his face. *I can't believe how this could happen.* He looks at Malek for help in understanding. No explanation comes.

The two rescuers, turned murderers, begin swimming back to shore, smiling as they go.

As they crawl out of the water and back on the wharf, Bob confronts them. He swallows a string of profanities, and in a voice thick and heavy, he demands, "Why did you do that?"

Obviously irritated, one of the two snorts, "Why don't you mind your own business?"

At the same time, a swell of rage rises in his partner's face. Mounting fury quickly tightens in his throat, overpowering him. The veins in his neck are pulsing. He scrunches his fingers, creating a furious, gnarled fist. He draws back that fist, intending to hit Bob.

He swings. In the twinkling of an eye, faster than anyone can see, Malek catches the man's fist. The man, in turn, tries to pull it back. It's stuck in the vice of Malek's hand. "You are an evil man," Malek declares in a thunderous voice. Then, he twists the man's fist until his forearm breaks.

The man screams, "Oh! Awe!"

As he holds his broken arm, the other man announces, "I oughta. . ."

Malek interrupts, "No, you ought to get out of here while you can."

THIRTY-SEVEN: YOU'RE THE PASTOR?

Faster than greased lightning, the roaring fire engulfs a nearby warehouse and then another. It won't stop until more than a dozen buildings are engulfed. Meanwhile, another burning ship slowly drifts out into the middle of the river.

As the last patient is loaded on Leroy's wagon, a reporter from the Missouri Gazette wants to take a picture of Leroy and run a story about his heroism. He refuses to be interviewed. "I was just one of several people who helped. Talk to some of the others."

Smiling half-heartedly, Bob says, "I'm proud of what you have done. Leroy, why not let him do a story about you?"

Red-faced, Leroy is chagrined as he shifts weight from one foot to another. Stammering slightly, he says, "I changed my name to Jerry." After allowing the two of them time to accept what he has said, he continues, "I am fearful my former employer, J. Gilbert Morningside, would find out where I am. Come on, there's still more work to do."

As they follow Jerry's wagon, carrying three more injured people, Bob's surprised when they arrive at a church building. It's a wood-framed building covered with dark tenting. A faded, amateurish sign over the front door says, "New Hope Church." Several patients from the explosion are already being treated inside.

A doctor and a young lady helper are working feverishly on them. It has a hospital scent, a combination of bleach and air freshener. All the activity surprises Bob. He's even more surprised when he asks Jerry, "Where's the pastor of this church?"

He's blown away by the bombshell Jerry drops. "He's right here; you are looking at him."

That answer is as unexpected as snow in the summer. Bob's anxious to hear when and why Jerry decided to become a pastor. He shares with him his misgivings, "You lack any theological education. How much do you know about being a pastor, how will you make a living, and what about denominational affiliation?"

Bob isn't prepared for Malek's comment. "Do you have the Book?" Jerry quickly produces his Bible. A short glance at it reveals it has been thoroughly used. Then, Malek says, "If you feel you have a calling and you have the Book, you have all you need." Then, he pauses and adds a word of caution, "You should expect there to be difficulties."

The lady helping the doctor looks up and recognizes Jerry. "Can you get us some water in a hurry," she asks.

Jerry mumbles, "I'll be right back."

Bob and Malek are left standing in a room with sixteen cots upon which patients are lying.

Some are severely burned and blackened. Others are bleeding copiously, giving off a coppery, metallic smell. Some patients have already gone into shock. Others are charred and blackened, with clothing melted into their skin. The stench of burnt flesh fills Bob's nostrils.

For him, it's a smell he will never forget. Not knowing how to help and not wanting to get in the way, they just stand there. This improvised hospital doesn't yet have a hospital smell, a combination of bleach and air freshener. However, the acrid, heavy scent of blood overrides everything.

Suddenly, a man enters the room behind them. He's heavy set, with a double chin and an unusually large nose. To Bob, there's something familiar about him, but he can't put his finger on it.

Clenching his jaw, he lets out a deep sigh and gives them the stare. Contempt is in his eyes. In a nasal tone that could freeze peas, he sneeringly says, "Well, at least this dump's serving some useful purpose." He shakes his head and hurriedly scans the room, and then says, "Doctor, I need you to come with me. We have some victims that are really bad off in my tavern." He shuffles over close to the doctor.

Not even bothering to look up, the doctor says, "I'll be there as soon as I can."

Pushing up his sleeves, the big man's voice is becoming even more harsh, as he snarls, "That wasn't a suggestion, Doc." The doctor glares at him and goes back to work.

The doctor's lady assistant rushes over to the man. Flames of anger leap through her. Her nostrils flare, and her pupils dilate. She yells, "Mister Remey, you need to leave right now."

Remey sniggers contemptuously, "You must be the sermonizer's old lady."

Before he can finish his thought, Jerry walks in with two buckets of water in his hands.

There's a pronounced edge in his voice as he asserts, "You need to get your sorry ass out of here, barkeep."

Clearly agitated, the man storms, "And are you going to make me?"

Before either one of them can say more, Malek speaks up, enunciating his words precisely, "He may not make you, but I will."

Remey studies Malek quickly but carefully. The man has a muscular build and stands well over six feet, with shoulder-length hair. He's free of emotion, totally composed, unruffled, and stone-faced. That face is imperturbable, no fear, no anger. He enunciates his words precisely, with little inflection. He is the epitome of cool. The look in his eyes is intimidating, and the man's voice could cut through granite. Remey decides to make a strategic retreat. Huffing and puffing, he storms away. A string of profanities spew from his mouth as he leaves.

After he leaves, Jerry says, "I see you met my wife, Neomi." He walks over and whispers something in Neomi's ear. Afterward, he returns to Bob and Malek and suggests, "I'd like to show the tavern owned by this man, Louis Remey. He migrated here from Alabama, and he brought three slaves with him. He doesn't like my kind of religion.

That's primarily because I'm not Catholic, and I'm opposed to slavery. One of my friends told me he was spreading stories about me being intimate with a free black woman here in town."

Malek jumps in, saying, "There's no truth in that."

"The man really works to discredit me every way he can and he has succeeded in turning several people against me as a preacher and my church." He pauses and puffs his cheeks out. "But I need to stay and help the doctor with Neomi."

Louis Remey

THIRTY-EIGHT: LOOKING OVER THE TOWN

Bob's telling himself, *A man doesn't get to see St. Louis when it was only a village.* Since Jerry and Neomi are busy, Malek and Bob decide to tour the small town. As they walk along, both of them feel a tension in the air. Bob is accustomed to saying, "Hello" or "How are you doing," when he encounters people. As they walk and meet others on the street, he offers a cheerful greeting, but they turn away with no response. Others they meet avoid them all together. It's off-putting. The buildings in town aren't any more friendly than the people.

From natural curiosity, Bob asks, "How did this town get started, anyway?"

Malek responds, "A few French settlers from the South brought African slaves with them here. Then, in 1817, five years before Jerry came here, *verily* steamboats replaced keelboats as the major travel vehicle on the Mississippi. *Thenceforth,* the town started to boom. *Methinks* you have heard about the Missouri Compromise?"

Bob nods his head. *I'd rather not go there; I don't want to talk about that period of history.*

Malek looks around him with an unsettling look in his eyes. He then says, "The next year, 1821, Missouri became a state, *verily,* a state where slavery is legal. Three years later, Jerry arrives, and *anon* joins the fight against slavery. The city was incorporated *nigh* two years ago, in 1822. *Erelong,* it experienced phenomenal growth due to its port connection with New Orleans."

Bob skips a step as he replies, "It doesn't look all that prosperous to me." *Look at those houses and those stores. Back home, we'd call this a ghetto.*

"You need to remember where we are," Malek declares. "*Thus,* in 1840, the population here will be seventy-seven thousand, eight hundred and sixty. In just ten years. in 1850, the population will be one hundred sixty thousand, which is bigger than New Orleans."

"Were any of my people in politics or river transportation?" Malek replies, "No, they were not."

"Does any of that have anything to do with my ancestors," Bob replies.

Imperturbable as usual, Malek over-enunciates, giving greater stress to every word. "Forsooth, is not that why we're here?" Staring directly into Bob's eyes, Malek says, "Most of these settlers have migrated *hither* from various parts of the South. *Methinks* almost a third of the people here now are slaves. They work on steamboats, warehouses, and taverns. *Mayhaps*, you see where this is going?"

Bob takes note of one of the few brick buildings in town. Malek looks at him knowingly as he says, "That is where we be headed."

THIRTY-NINE:
SCRUMPTIOUS

As they get closer to the two-story building, Bob can read a faded sign saying, "Bull & Ring Tavern." When they get inside, Bob's jaw drops as he does a double take. The extraordinarily large room has a unique ambiance. The air is rich with the scents of food, smoke, and rum. At several different tables, men are having spirited discussions. They might even be called debates. At other tables, men are playing poker. A full bar area is against the south wall. A small combo is in one corner, consisting of a banjo, piano, and a fiddle. The song they're currently doing is "Home Sweet Home." The atmosphere is vibrant, with a few couples dancing around frivolously. Meals are served at a single, long table, where Malek and Bob find a seat.

The meal consists of ham, sausage, butter, boiled potatoes, pies and cider. Bob's thinking, *I hope there's no limit to how much you can eat.* Malek's verdict is, "The food is delicious and tasty."

Bob responds, "You can say that again. It's "Scrumptious and yummy."

After eating, Malek checks on a room for the night. He and Bob are amused when they're told a bed is one price and a pallet on the floor is half that amount.

They find it hard to sleep, even in a bed, with all the noise downstairs. The next morning finds them at the home of Jerry and Neomi for breakfast. Wife and mother, Neomi, turns out to be a remarkable person. She's friendly and energetic. She's sorta pretty, sorta not, but she has soft, feminine curves. Bob's impressed with her red hair and green eyes. A sweet female scent emanates from her when she walks by. "Well, what do you think of our town." She asks.

Bob hesitates a moment, hoping Malek will answer. Finally, he says, "It's interesting."

She laughs at his answer and goes about her business.

As they're eating, a little fellow joins them, rubbing his eye. "Good morning, Louis," she says. "Malek and Bob, I want you to meet our older son."

Bob smiles at the delightful little fellow. He extends both arms in welcome to him, but he continues to prefer his mother's embrace. Bob has taken another bite of bacon, when Malek declares, "Tell us about your abolitionist activities."

Jerry's face is quickly covered in a bright shade of red. He stares at his wife intently. An unsettling feeling is clearly welling up inside her and him both. There's a nervous tremor in his voice as he says, "I don't know what you mean."

Bob steps in, "Come on, Jerry, you know who we are. Malek already knows all about it. No way can you keep stuff from him."

Malek intrudes, "We know about your friend, Elijah Parish Lovejoy, the Presbyterian Minister here, the tract he published, and how you helped him restore his printing press after it was destroyed twice. *Howbeit*, two years from now, they will try again. This time, they will surely succeed in destroying his printing press and killing him."

A frown and a fearful look comes on both of their faces. Bob repeats, "I told you he knows stuff."

Malek continues, "*Nother* thing you know not what John Brown will say publicly, after Lovejoy's death, 'Here before God in the presence of these witnesses, from this time, I concentrate my life to the destruction of slavery.'"

Tears are streaming down Neomi's face. She says, "Will this awful evil of slavery ever end?"

Malek answers, "Indeed it will, but at an unbelievable cost."

Bob tries to put her at ease, "Trust me, in years to come, what you two are doing will be applauded as heroic and admirable." With that, Jerry takes his wife in his arms, offering comfort.

The scene changes as a second little fellow enters the room. Jerry explains, "This bodacious fellow is Jeremiah, our younger son." With that, Larry grabs a slice of bacon from Bob's plate, holds it in his mouth, and runs around the table. Bob gets up and chases him around, then grabs and hugs him.

When the two of them settle down, Jerry opens up, "I will never forget what you two did for me back in Tennessee. I had no idea what I would do or where. Then, I met Neomi shortly after I arrived, and soon after, I discovered what real love is. Both of us are committed to serving the God we love." Neomi wraps her arms around him in sympathetic agreement.

"It seems to me life is difficult here," Bob says. "Why is that?"

Jerry explains, "As you know, Missouri is a slave state, while across the river, Illinois is a free state. That means any slave who can manage to get across the river will be free, as all men should be free."

Mounting exasperation is tightening Bob's throat as he asks. "What about this character, Louis Remy? What's his problem?"

Jerry looks at his wife, and she nods her head, saying, "Um, huh." He then says, "Come with me; I want to show you something." So, they leave the house. In a matter of minutes, he says, "Yesterday, I was too busy." In a matter of minutes, they're standing in front of a different tavern. Jerry explains, "They won't be very busy this time of day."

FORTY: WORSHIP INTERRUPTED

The building is constructed in the *poteau sur sol* (post on foundation) method. Inside the main room, there is a noxious and putrid odor. They have barely entered the room when two ladies, indecently dressed, ask them, "Want to party?" Jerry pushes them away. No one is eating at the long table, but several men are standing around a roulette wheel. The long bar has four men tipping more than a few. There are no women customers, there are no stimulating discussions, and there are no dancers. There is a man with a guitar accompanying a singer-dancer doing a poor rendition of "Jump Jim Crow." He isn't very good, and the song is probably liked by no one except the performers. Two men are slugging it out in one corner. Nobody's paying any attention to them as it isn't much of a fight. BLAT! Howling. Clunk.

Malek says, "I have seen enough." With that, they turn and leave. On the way back to Jerry's, Malek asks, "When are you making your next river crossing?"

Running his fingers through his hair, Jerry appears fidgety. Still, he answers, "Tomorrow, Sunday night."

Bob's fired up. Smacking his lips, he says, "Can we go with you? Please." Jerry makes no reply, but he is bouncing on his toes.

On Sunday morning, Bob's surprised as folding chairs have been set up in front of the church building since the church is still filled with those injured from the steamboat explosion. Bob's experiencing a measure of pride as he listens to his forefather say, "Love is the fairest flower that blooms in God's garden. And love is the hardest lesson to learn in Christianity." It feels good for Bob to identify with the preacher as he listens empathetically. Other members of the gathered congregation are enjoying the sweet and pleasant message.

Out of the blue, there's another voice. A booming, angry voice is shouting, "Do you religious nuts not read the newspaper?" Then a shot is fired, BOOM!

Panic replaces warm, sympathetic emotions. All over are blinking eyes, fearful and pale faces. There is also an abundance of trembling and shaking. Unseen on the surface, but accelerated heart rates and rapid breathing are all around.

Like everybody else in the congregation, Bob looks around to see who's interrupting this worship service. Rage is nearly consuming him, it's the man he met yesterday. It's Louis Remy himself. Two men are with him. The one on the left is busily reloading. The one on is right, is waving his weapon about threateningly. Clenching a copy of the Missouri Gazette, Remy roars, "In Virginia, a black slave named Nat Turner, has led a rebellion. It was the deadliest insurrection in the country's history." He is now breathless with rage. "Those blood-thirsty animals slaughtered men, women and children. Hundreds of people were murdered in cold blood. And it's spreading all over the South. For all I know, his followers are plotting right here to kill all whites."

Jerry speaks up in an excited tone, "You need to leave right now. This is a worship service!"

With his face red and slobbers on his lips, he screams, "Before we go, we're gonna kill that black scum sitting right over there!" He points his finger at a member of Jerry's congregation. Clearly terrified and petrified, the man's eyes are rapidly blinking.

Both men, with Remey, are hulking large, and both are wearing scowls. They sweep their guns so that they point to everyone soon or late. Remey has a pistol in his hand and swings it about in a menacing manner.

All three guns can fire only one shot before it must be reloaded. Before the men can actually use their weapons, Malek is on his feet. He has a hand pointed at each of the two men. Harnessing the power of his mind to control electricity. He uses an electrical ray from his brain to the guns.

The first man fires. BOOM! The entire barrel explodes. It looks like a bent yard rake.

The charcoal-like whiff of gunpowder is strong in all their nostrils. The second man fires.

BOOM! That barrel also explodes. The biting smell of gunpowder is even more intense. It is bold, sharp, and strong.

In a calm, almost monotone voice, Malek says, "Unless you want the same thing to happen to you, you'll throw down those defunct guns and get away from here."

Both men throw down their dysfunctional weapons and leave in a dead run. Remy isn't far behind them, chump, thump, wheeze.

Jerry calms his nerves and clears his throat. No more small repetitive movements. He's back to breathing normally and standing proud. He continues. "What that man didn't say about Nat Turner is he and his followers used, as weapons, knives, axes and hoe handles. They were defeated by three companies of artillery. Right or wrong, Nat Turner was a deeply religious man."

The rest of the service is uneventful. Still, there is a sense of apprehension in the air, felt by everyone present. Bob is reflecting, like everyone else, *I am closer to death than I have realized.*

FORTY-ONE: LOOKING AHEAD

When they're alone in a quiet moment, Bob asks the Defender, "Which one of Jerry's two boys is my ancestor?"

After taking a few steps, Malek answers, "Ye can be *sore* proud of both of those boys. Both follow their father into the ministry. When the Civil War comes, President Lincoln, also from Illinois announces a call for soldiers. They both serve in the Union Army. Gregg serves as a chaplain in the 13th Illinois, and Louis becomes a Captain of Infantry in the 21st Illinois. Both men survive the war and return to the pastorate. *Yea,* both will be good men, but Louis is your ancestor.

Speaking of good men, one of Jerry's grandsons, and *thine* ancestor, will not be such a good man. *Forsooth,* he will be a *peterman.*"

Bob goes stone-faced; he winces and swallows hard. "Will you tell me about him?"

"Gregg has three sons and two daughters. The second son, Timothy, is *nay beef-witted* but is a very intelligent individual. The problem is he is also *sore* lazy. He could have done anything he wanted to in life, *howbeit* he didn't want to work at anything. He marries *thrice* and cheats on all three of them. He will be a good-looking fellow. He will be well-built, what you call ripped. He'll be *bereft* of even an ounce of fat. But he's pretty *scurvy. Wherefore,* he tries several scams. He will drift into a town and pretend to be sick and depressed. The reason changes from place to place. After he tells a few strategic people he plans to take his own life, folks take up a collection to help him. When he gets the money, he slips out of town. But finally, he comes up with a better con. He starts passing counterfeit money. *Bethink,* during the Civil War, *forsooth,* banks issued their own currency. *Betimes,* Tim prints his own bills issued by a non-existent bank. *Behold,* he was one of your forefathers."

FORTY-TWO:
CON MAN

The starless and moonless sky is pitch-dark. It's also dreadfully ghoulish. The water is dark as a nightmare or a bad dream as they silently work the oars on the small boat. They carry no light with them, which is dangerous in and of itself. A scattering of piddling lights shine across the broad expanse. Bob and Malek are about to help Jerry as he delivers a black family to escape to Illinois and freedom.

Everyone on board is more than a little antsy. Of course, all members of the group are constantly looking around, checking for danger. Mother, Dad, and little Benjamin, the three members of a black family, are motionless. When they move, their movements are stiffened. Intense fear shows on all three faces. Their pupils are dilated. Their mouths are dry, and they're feeling jittery.

The adrenaline spikes in Bob. Somehow, this experience is becoming more of an adventure than he had imagined. Pictures of what could be now flash in his mind. They include injury or death for him and the others in this small boat. Malek is his normal, matter-of-fact self. He's as unimpassioned as usual. By contrast, Jerry, who has made this trip several times before, even so, he is shaking or trembling.

At a point where Jerry estimates they are about halfway across the river, a moving light shows up. It appears to be a couple hundred yards away from them. In this situation, it's impossible to know what it is or how far away it may be. Even more fear rolls in like a massive dark storm cloud. Bob notices his hands are getting clammy. He can also hear others in the boat praying. Everyone continues to look around. That's when it looks as if a light is approaching them.

Unexpectedly, Bob feels a small hand reach out to hold onto him. He holds the little boy close. Then he says, "You hold onto me. I have help row too." His arms soon are growing weary from rowing but he can't stop. He experiences difficulty breathing and his heart is beating faster.

Suddenly, that light goes off. Bob can't be sure if that's a good thing or a bad thing. He takes a deep breath and puffs out his cheeks. A thought comes tripping, uninvited, into his mind. *What if I never see Belinda again? She may never know what happened to me.*

Wonder if she knows how much I love her? Somehow, all other questions become trivial or inconsequential.

In a soft voice, having a tint of apprehension, Jerry says, "Just a few more miles, and we've got it made." The deserted shore is now visible through the darkness. Faint lights scattered about on the land are comforting.

All of a sudden, Bob hears the sound of voices coming toward them. The little boy hugs close to him. He tries to conceal his growing apprehension. He is relieved when he can see the faces that go with the voices. They're also black.

As the black family steps out of the boat and onto solid ground, they're filled with heartfelt gratefulness. The husband bends over and kisses the Illinois soil. Tears come to his eyes as he mutters, "Freedom…precious freedom." He and his wife both hug Jerry, Malek, and Bob. As the three of them push off from the shore, he says, "Thank you for making all our dreams come true."

As Bob joins his two friends rowing again, the angle of his chin is up. His shoulders are upright and slightly aback. A sense of pride and happiness washes over him. In his mind, an uplifting thought drifts through. *I have achieved something tremendously important.*

FORTY-THREE: FEARFUL RIVER CROSSING

The return trip back across the river is much less stressful since their cargo has been delivered. Bob's eyebrows are relaxed, his head's back, and his chin's up. The sound of the rushing river ever gurgling is both haunting and mesmerizing. In the distance is the familiar sound of a whistle on a stern-wheeler. His feeling of being as satisfied as a big sunflower is short-lived however. A reception committee awaits them on shore.

Rowing into a small cove, they're surprised to see three lanterns before them. Bob wonders, *Could it be night-fisherman?* Jerry whispers to them, "Get ready, boys, we've got trouble ahead."

Agreeing with him, without saying a word verbally, Malek sends, *I'm afeared nowise* is *this reception a good thing.*

Turns out, Louis Remey's standing on a small dock. His arms are crossed; his nostrils are flared, and he's boiling with indignation. Rage is flooding through his veins as he spews a string of profanities. His voice is whisky-soaked. Flames of anger are leaping through him.

Loud and obstructive. Both the man on his left and on his right have guns at the ready. Both are large fellows, even bigger and meaner looking than Ramey had with him this morning.

Bob's wondering, *Where does he get these guys?*

Totally passionless, Malek offers a few words as soft as rain. "Gentlemen, what is it you think you're doing here?"

Remey snarls, "We know what you're doing, and we are here to. . . ."

Malek steps closer to the little man, stabs him with his forefinger, and says, "What we are doing here is none of *thine* business." Then, he turns to the man on his left. This man has a musky odor about him and a bushy head of hair. He's also muscle-bound and towering over others.

With a voice free of emotion and almost no inflection, Malek says, "I see you came up with a different gun from your friends this morning." His words could cut through granite.

The big guy sneers at Malek, and with a half-smile, he lifts one corner of his mouth. With absolute contempt, he stares at the man who is even taller than he is.

Malek fixes his eyes on the man's weapon. With super-human strength, he draws the rifle out of the man's hand. The man lacks the sufficient strength to resist. Malek takes the gun in his hands and studies it. "Model 1803 Harper's Ferry Musket," he casually says.

Taking the gun by the barrel, he swings it and smashes it into the man's face. Next, he draws his knee and breaks the gun in half over it. The big man falls to the ground, holding his bleeding face.

Remy can't believe how this could happen. Fear begins running through his veins. His eyes widen, and he shakes his head as the man with the broken nose gets up from the ground. Malek turns to the other man, saying, "You're next."

That man looks at Remy. His bloated face goes pale as Malek's eyes bore into him. Then, a strange look envelopes his face. He throws his rifle to the ground and runs as fast as he can. Huffing and heaving, his saliva tastes like copper.

Jerry smiles at Louis Remy. He doesn't say anything but he does nod his head. At this point, Remy sighs rather loudly, shakes his head, and then walks away.

At breakfast the next morning, Malek offers words of encouragement, "Situations do not define who we are." He pauses a moment. His facial expression doesn't change, but the tone of his voice does. In a silvery tone, clear, light, and pleasant, he says, "All things work together for good to them that love the Lord." He doesn't explain any further.

Bob also tries to encourage them. "What you're doing is important. Keep on keeping on."

Malek interrupts him, "In a few days, the news will hit about a gold strike at Pikes Peak will cause Louis Remy and his friends will leave for the gold fields."

Jerry asks, "Are you sure?"

Bob answers the question with, "I told you, he knows stuff."

Jerry can't wait to share this bit of news with his wife. The news cheers her soul, and she becomes dizzy with excitement. Both of them experience a surge of happiness and celebrate all day.

Back on the road, Malek is looking for a place where they can time travel, without being seen by others. As they move along, admiring the "Mighty Mississippi," Bob poses an unexpected question. "Do you know anything about Huntington's Disease?"

Malek waits a couple of minutes and then rolls his eyes before articulating, "Some of the symptoms of Huntington's Disease include tremors, slow or abnormal eye movements. Some of the other symptoms include depression, irritability, and suicidal thoughts. There are a few more symptoms."

Into Bob's mind come thoughts with which he still isn't at peace. Somberly, he asks, "What about the life expectancy of a person with that disease?"

With genuine empathy in his tone, Malek answers, "When the illness is recognized at your age, life expectancy should be between twenty and thirty more years."

After a moment's silence, Bob repeats, somewhat joyfully, "Thirty years? Hmmm."

His mind is frolicking through a Springtime meadow.

FORTY-FOUR: REPULSIVE RECEPTION

Malek is now waxing eloquently, "On May 17, 1875, forsooth the same day as the first Kentucky Derby. Bruce Bancroft is verily excited about his date tonight with Shirley Harshall. Her eyes are audacious blue, and her body's unbelievable, for him. This is their third date, but he has decided the first time they went out that this was the one for him. *Yea*, her face is like a morning in the springtime, and when she smiles, her entire face lights up. He has decided he's going to ask her to marry him. He's so excited he's unable to be still."

Bob responds with a question, "And this guy is an ancestor of mine?"

With a cold emptiness in his voice, Malek says, "To be sure, he's Owen's son. Of course, Owen never had anything to do with him. Alas, you remember Owen was married three times and cheated on all of them. Bruce was the son of the first wife. Ere their first anniversary, she divorced him." Without pause or hesitation, Malek returns to his story. "The two of them, Bruce and Shirley, are sitting on the porch swing, at her house. Nervously, he says, 'I was wondering if you would like to spend the rest of your life with me?'"

"She looks shocked. 'Do you mean get married,' she asks."

"'That's what I mean,' he responds."

Bob nods his head in wry approval. With anxious expectation, he leans in closer to her, rubbing hands together.

Malek's enjoying his tale, but he won't allow his face to illustrate that fact. He continues, "She rolls her eyes and crosses her arms. Then, she starts playing with her hair. In a shaky voice, she says, 'Bruce, you're a good man and a lot of fun, but I can't marry you. When I get married, it will be to a man of means. You're a school dropout. You'll never amount to anything. I'm sorry.'"

Bob's lower jaw drops, and horizontal wrinkle lines form on forehead. He says, "Oh, man. Aw." He's bummed out and goes stone-faced.

Malek's voice is free of emotion as he continues, "As you can imagine, a dizzying sense of disappointment sweeps over Bruce. He feels like the bottom fell out of his world. His stomach drops, and he has a sudden feeling of nausea."

Bob's shoulders are slumped as he shakes his head. When Malek asks if he would like to check on Bruce a few years down the road, his only response is rubbing the back of his neck. His mind is bombarded with arresting thoughts. *How will this guy deal with this disappointment? I think I know how he feels. At least he's not a crook like his Dad.* Here and now, he asks Malek, "What does he do next?"

FORTY-FIVE: DEALING WITH DISAPPOINTMENT

After staring silently into the blue for a minute or two, Malek says, "Broken-hearted, he ambles from place to place, always moving west. He works here and there at various jobs, nothing of any consequence. Being home sick adds to his discomfort. Finally, he settles in Arbrow, OK., where he works for a local wagon-maker and wheelwright."

They don't discuss it, but Bob and Malek agree to time travel to Arbrow a few years in the future. Bob is slow to recognize it, but they communicate subliminally. Their emotions are transferred back and forth without language or words, only vibrating energy.

Using duration control, Malek once again bends time. While he is capable of folding a century into a scant few minutes and taking 365,000 sunrises and an equal number of sunsets and compressing them into a handful of seconds, this time, they are only tripping a couple of hundred miles and a handful of years. In the blink of an eye, they are there. Bob calls it, "In the bat of an eye."

They have barely arrived when they encounter a young man with curly brown hair, dressed casually. The plaid shirt has a torn sleeve, and the jeans have oil or some kind of stain on them. A large, long-haired, dog is walking at his side. Bob says, "Wonder what kind of dog that is."

Malek says, matter-of-factly, "It's a Labrador Retriever, and his name is "Juneo."

The man's nose is bold, bony, and chiseled. His nut-brown eyes are sunken in sockets, with crow's feet at the sides. He's tall and very muscular. When he gets closer, they see the corners of his mouth are curved up. There's also a twinkle in his eyes. When they get within speaking distance, Bob says, "How you doing these days?"

That slight smile spreads over his face as he says, "To tell you the truth I'm happy as a pig in the mud." Laughter shows on his face. "I've been trying for weeks to talk to this girl I'm interested in. Just now, she actually talked to me."

Malek jumps in with, "Congratulations, Bruce." He thanks him as he walks away. They watch him as he heads in the direction of the wagon shop.

When he's out of earshot, Bob casually remarks, "It would be nice to know who the girl is."

"The girl is Molly Banton," Malek says, "she works in her father's store down the street."

Bob responds, "Do you think so?"

In a penetrating voice, which makes Bob a little uncomfortable, Malek pronounces, "I don't think; I know. She is goodly, you would say pert and pretty, of average size, with long, brown hair. She is soft-spoken and very particular about what she wears. Though nobody knows about it, she has a cacophonic fear of ugliness. Most importantly, she is a born again believer. Not only does she talk the talk, but she walks the walk."

FORTY-SIX:
A BULLY GETS HIS

This afternoon, Bob and Malek are in the general store where Molly works. Her father is out of the store. He's probably fishing somewhere, which he often does when business is slow. Another customer is also in the store. Judging by his appearance and his smell, the man is a mule-skinner. At least, he surely smells like one. Bob and Malek try to stay upwind from him. He also has a full beard and a dusty, dismal hat that looks as if he wore it across the continent and back.

"Kin I see those shirts that are on the top shelf," the man says. Molly gets the obligatory ladder and climbs up two steps. The muleskinner says, "Here, let me help you." With that, he puts both his hands on her hips.

A swell of rage rises in her face. In a clamorous, loud voice, she snarls, "Take your hands off me."

He replies, "Now, Missy, I was just trying to be helpful. He, he."

Down from the ladder, she hurriedly starts back toward her normal position behind the counter. She's stopped by a hand on her shoulder. It's a hand, dirty as a pair of oxen at the end of a workday. The man with the beard is demanding, "Show me a new pair of boots, Cutie." She removes his hand sternly. She blows out her cheeks as her nostrils flare. With her eyebrows lowered she says, "Keep your hands off me."

In a whisper, Bob says, "Shouldn't we do something?"

Malek doesn't respond. Instead, he nods toward the front of the store and Bruce, who has just appeared in the store.

Molly hurries back to get a counter between herself and this rude customer and his inappropriate advances. As she turns her back on the man, he grabs her buttock with both hands and laughs, "Ha, haw!"

Molly jerks around and slaps the man. BLAT! Mounting exasperation tightens in her throat. She clenches her fists, and her face goes red.

The muleskinner continues to laugh. He says, "I love a woman with spunk." With that, he grabs both of her shoulders.

Faster than a chasing cheetah, Bruce is behind the man. "Take your hands off of her," he demands.

The bearded man blinks rapidly, trying to process what this stranger has said. In a soft, yet manly voice, Bruce says, "The lady wants you to back off."

The muleskinner feels a rash of rage rising in him. Judging by his face, fury is surging through him. He growls, "Why don't you mind your own business, spoke-maker!" without hesitation, he swings his fist.

Bruce ducks faster than a hummingbird's wing. As he does, he slams his fist into the insolent character's gut. KLAM! The dusty man staggers backward. Bruce quickly stands to his feet. He hammers his fist into the bearded man's face. SMACK!

The man falls to the floor. FA-THUD!

Bruce helps the man to his feet. Then, he grabs his shoulder and forcibly ushers him out of the store. Next, he grins at Molly, saying, "I guess you lost one customer."

Then and there, Molly's body language changes abruptly. She employs different smiles as she talks with Bruce. Not only that, she also listens to him, for the first time.

The polite but congenial conversation brings a smile to Bob's face. Malek's lips are set in a thin line, impassive with no hint of emotion. They pay for the snacks for which they came into the store. As they turn to leave, Bob winks at Bruce.

Back out on the street, Bob and Malek are discussing what just transpired. Bob shares an observation, "I guess Bruce made a real impression on Molly."

After a moment of solemn silence, Malek says, "I would say he surely did. You should hear what she says to the Sheriff in the morning."

Bob's eyebrows go high and curve. He blinks rapidly, trying to process. "You can't possibly know what she will say tomorrow."

Malek rolls his eyes and looks out into nothingness. Then he asserts, "Horokinesis is accessing, experiencing and influencing events in the past, present and/or future. Time shifting can only be achieved with the help of an expediter, such as myself. Would you be interested in what Molly's going to tell the Sheriff?"

In Molly's velvety voice, unbelievably smooth and soft, Malek says, "Sheriff, you will not believe what happened in the store yesterday. This man came in and started taking liberties with me, and he wouldn't quit..."

"At this point, Sheriff Gregg Albright interrupts her, 'I already know what Bruce Bancroft did; how he knocked out that fellow and then ushered him to the door. It's all over town."

At this point, he goes back to Molly's honeyed and pleasant voice, "It was wonderful. I never knew how amazing that man was. Take it from me: Bruce isn't afraid of anything or anybody."

Then, in Malek's own voice, he says, "The Sheriff is thinking Bruce might just be the man I'm looking for to be my part-time deputy. I'm going to ask him. My arthritis is killing me."

Sheriff Bruce Barton

FORTY-SEVEN: A RAILROAD EVEN

Immediately, Bob recognizes the weather is cloudy and overcast. And there's also a strong breeze. Malek says, "It is *nowise* strong enough to pull the feathers off of a chicken, as people say around here. But it seems to be building." It doesn't take any intuition or meteorological knowledge or intuition to recognize rain's on the way. The air is extremely humid. As perspiration begins to form on his arms, Bob remarks, "Looks like we'll be right in the middle of a rainstorm."

After he has had time to look around, he enquires of Malek, "Are you sure we're in the right place? This doesn't look like the town we left two minutes ago." The town is bigger, more than twice the size of the former version. The town is busier, with people coming and going, talking, laughing, and yelling, "You want to get out of my way." It is also more commercial, buying, selling, gambling, and drinking. Beyond that, something dark or gloomy permeates the air.

Malek's face is blank and vacant. His eyes have an unusual color, violet, with more red in them than blue. His chin obtrudes like a unicorn's horn. Bob is very familiar with Malek enunciating his words precisely, with little inflection. Unfortunately, he is also very familiar with how Malek can remain silent and refuse to respond at all. That's what he does this time.

I'll just use my own deductive ability to figure this out, he muses. The first thing he concentrates on is anew train station and the railroad running beside it. On the end of the station building is "Arbow, OK." *I guess this is the right place. I'll figure out the when later.*

The question on Bob's mind is: "Did Bruce and Molly marry?"

Malek replies, "Yes, they did. They now have three children, and he's the Sheriff here."

As they move closer to the railroad Bob enquires, "What's the deal with these cross streets? They weren't here before. And what do you know about this railroad?"

It takes Malek a while before he responds. "The railroad is the Atchison, Topeka, and Santa Fe. Laying the rails has progressed to about ten miles south of here. All of these new streets are a reflection of how much the town has grown. The cross streets are A, B, and C, while the streets parallel to Main are Butternut and Oak." As they move toward Main Street, Bob takes note of the cobblestone street. Malek explains, "They aren't really cobblestone. The stones are rounded and smooth, but they are of various sizes. They are set in sand, but only parts of some streets are paved. There's still plenty of dust,"

Malek calls attention to the dentist's office, which is no longer a part of the barbershop, and a new, three-storied building where the burned-out building was before. A sign out front indicates there's a doctor's office somewhere inside.

A few steps later, the rain begins to fall softly. The first saloon they come to, here on Main, is now expanded. It has a large false front with the name "Jake's Place" emblazoned on it.

An earthy, yeasty scent of old beer flows through the door. Bob pauses a moment, listening to the piano player. *I should know that song; it sounds familiar,* Bob reflects.

Though no oral words have passed between them, Malek answers, "'I'll Take You Home Again, Kathleen,'" by Wetendorf."

Cracks of lightning are now ripping across the sky. The rain has changed to a gray drizzle.

FORTY-EIGHT: STORM'S ON THE WAY

Next to Jake's Place is another store with a large sign declaring, William's General Store." A couple of wagons and teams are parked in front of it. One of them is pulled by a pair of oxen. Those oxen are feeling jittery or nervous due to the rain.

Bob asks, "Where's the church?"

In a voice like ice water, Malek says, "The only church in town is a quarter of a mile away from other establishments. It looks just like it did when we were here last time, except the graveyard has expanded significantly. *Howbeit*, the preacher still doesn't live here. He comes to town every second and fourth Sunday."

Bob's perplexed. "The town has grown, but the church hasn't?"

Malek's answer is a simple, "Forsooth."

Directly opposite of them, within spitting distance, is the wagon-builder's shop. Adjacent to it is the blacksmith's shop. Both have large open areas. A hammer against an anvil rings out. Blam! Blam! Blam! Bob has interested eyes. His pupils dilate, taking in the blacksmith's work. He's fascinated.

Bob scratches his head and asks, "Wasn't there a bordello right there?"

Malek admits there was and explains, "It hasn't gone very far; now it's on Oak Street."

Another one of several surprises is the general store, now called "Wilson's Merchandise."

It now occupies what before was two separate buildings. Bob remarks, "Their business must be doing well." Two wagons are parked in front. People are coming and going out of the store, even in the rain falling in a gray drizzle.

It isn't long before pinpricks of rain are stinging their skin and slapping them in the face. The dry earth drinks in the cool rain. "Wait," Bob says. "What's that?" A stone building on the corner of Main and B Street houses a bank. Actually, a stone building, carefully constructed, has a voguish appearance. "That's a real sign of growth," Bob pronounces. "I don't know about the bank's name though, "Prosperity National Bank."

This part of the street hasn't been introduced to cobblestone, or whatever they call their cheap imitation. The recently dust-covered street is now muddy and slushy, thanks to the pelting rain.

The two visitors are standing under a portico to stay out of the rain. A wagon, pulled by two mules, is rumbling by them. Mud and sludgy water are splashed on both of them. Bob roars, "Aw! Come on!"

Both of them decide this would be a good time to stop in the Sheriff's Office. Once there, a young man greets them with, "I'm Deputy Ben Raystat. What can I do for you?"

Malek responds, "We want to talk to Bruce. Is he in?"

The deputy responds politely. "He's in his office, right this way."

Bob is reflecting. *I see they now have a jail here, and the sheriff has his own office. Must have built it on the back.*

Bruce is delighted to see them, though he's surprised that neither one of them looks like they have aged any. The three of them talk about his and Molly's three children, about the church they attend. And he tells them about his life as a full-time sheriff. "The problem is my reputation seems to be growing every year that passes."

Bob jumps in with, "That's a good thing; isn't it?" For a moment or so, he reflects on the cowboy lawmen he has always idolized: Wyatt Earp, Wild Bill Hickok, Pat Garrett, and others. *I have a famous lawman as a forefather. Fantastic.*

Out of the blue, the sheriff's face has a hang-dog expression. His eyes narrow, and he looks downward. His shoulders slump as he says, "Stories keep being passed around that I am some kind of superfast gun hand. I have never been a gunslinger. The way I figure it, I can't outdraw these bad men, so I don't try. I outright shoot them or bang them over the head. But lately, I've been dealing with back-shooters, and that's another matter. Sooner or later, some villainous louts are going to get me."

Mild disillusionment creeps into Bob's mind. *In the short time I have known this man, to whom I'm actually related, I have come to deeply admire him. Now, he appears to be afraid.*

What Bruce says next shocks him even more. Looking directly at Malek, he says, "I know who and what you are."

What could he possibly mean by that? Bob muses.

Without hesitation, Bruce looks directly at Malek and asks, "Would it be possible for me to talk to you alone?"

Of course, Bob wonders, *What's going on?* But he says, "I'll go and check out the school. I wanted to see it anyway. I'll be back in a few minutes." With that, he heads for the door.

When he has left the room, Bruce says, "Molly and I spent a lot of time figuring out who you were. We know what you are and where you come from. The thing is, I need your help and wisdom. My wife is dearly afraid someone is going to come into town and kill me. But if we leave, what will I do? How will we survive?"

Malek is silent for a while. His face appears guarded and impassive, with no hint of feelings. His chiseled chin is lifted. His eyes bore into Bruce's soul. His voice has a cold emptiness, but he enunciates his words precisely. "Yes, I am a celestial agent, and yes, I have a genuine interest in you. *Methink*s you would be wise to relocate and take up a different profession."

The rest of his words are canceled by several gunshots. BLAM! BLAM! BLAM! BLAM!

FORTY-NINE:
TRAVELING FAR FROM HOME

Bob is walking back down Main Street. He's noticing all the people out on the street, men and women, in the rain no less. In addition, there are several children playing in the street, in mud puddles more specifically. He stops to watch them play and laugh. *The rain doesn't seem to bother them. It bothers me, though.*

All of a sudden, two men are running out of the bank. Pelting rain greets them. With guns drawn, they start shooting randomly. People scream and yell. Everyone runs for cover. The two men hurdle onto waiting horses. WHINNI! The third man's already mounted. NEIGH! At the same time, shooting. BLAM! BLAM! They're shooting randomly, BLAM! BLAM! BLAM! SNORT! The smoky smell runs through the area even in the rain.

A little kid runs toward Bob, yelling, "No, no." SPLISH! SPLASH! KATHUD! He stumbles and falls. Bob runs toward him.

GALLOPITY-GLOP! SPLASH! The bandits are hard to watch in the pouring rain. However, it's easy to hear the sound of them escaping the town.

Suddenly, Bob feels excruciating pain. *It's in my chest.* It's g*etting worse and worse. I can't stand it!* That searing hurt feels like hot oil running through his veins. He grits his teeth, trying to push through it. Then, a numbing cold creeps up his legs. He drops to the ground, with his face in the sloppy mud. Then and there, total darkness engulfs him. Next, there's a horrible choking sensation. He's becoming weak. Everything goes black. *I have never felt this way before,* he thinks. Suddenly, *The hurt's all gone.*

He's moving. *I'm not walking.* Trying to reorient himself to his surroundings he can't help wondering where all the people went. The world is quickly passing away from him. He's moving through some kind of translucent shaft. No way he can ascertain how fast; there's no wind force or vibration. *It's like an outer space 3-D movie,* he surmises.

Suddenly, he's joined by a fellow traveler. There, moving beside him, is Malek, who lays a gentle hand on Bob's shoulder. Within a short while, they come to land once again. Malek offers a simple but less-than-satisfying explanation. You are in a different dimension.

Instantly, after they set foot on solid ground, Bob is amazed and thrilled with what he sees all around him. Ruby-like and sapphire-colored flowers are literally everywhere. The colors are vivid beyond imagination, each one dazzling in its own way. He's astonished at the hundreds of brilliant butterflies airborne among them. Wonderous trees of various kinds and descriptions have leaves like emeralds. The air is fresh and clean, like an early morning in the Spring. Bob has trouble taking it all in and wrapping his head around the question, *Where am I? It's astounding. Fantastic.* Ahead of them, now coming into view, is a magnificent city. No beauty ever beheld by human eye compares to the splendor he is seeing.

Turning to Malek, he asks, "Do you hear that music?"

In a calm, restrained voice, Malek says, "You haven't heard anything yet."

Bob's becoming more and more exuberant. He has never felt so wondrously joyful. *I have never seen a place like this before. Everything's so beautiful. The colors are fabulous; bright and glorious. I never saw colors like this before. Even the road, under our feet, glows with a glowing luster.*

Then Malek takes Bob by the hand and says, "Time for another trip."

FIFTY:
IS THIS THE END?

Malek and Bob time-travel once again. But this time he's traveling from another universe and a different dimension. As accustomed as he has become to phenomenal travel, this journey is even more astonishing. Bob's stunningly amazed by the process. What he sees is hard to define. Colors of every hue, are tumbling wildly past him. Bright and dark streaks fly by. Blurred images of stars and galaxies stream past him. *How can all of this be happening? Can I believe my eyes when my other senses do nothing to confirm? For that matter, I'm not sure what's happening.*

Suddenly, Bob begins another transition. The sense of wonderment gives way to confusion. Dazzling radiance is overtaken by frightening confusion. The shimmer is gone. So is the joyfulness. He hears a peculiar voice, "Bob." It sounds way off somewhere. "Bob, can you hear me?"

Bob opens his eyes to see Doctor Clements bending over him. The doctor says, "We thought we had lost you." A chill freezes the doctor in place. Horizontal wrinkle lines form on his forehead. It's easy to see the man is surprised. The man's eyes water or shine with disbelief. There in then, his mouth splits open wide in a booming laugh.

Within a few days, Bob is back up, walking around again. The bank-robbers have been caught. Two of them are even now in jail. The third one was killed during the capture. Bob gets to know the Sheriff's family. Doing so gives him a sense of satisfaction. *That's my family, he tells himself more than two dozen times.*

At this point, it's time to make another trip. The thrill of supernatural time travel is just as thrilling this time as it was the first time. Bob tells himself, *I'll never get tired of this, never*. He fully expects to return to where he was before returning here to Oklahoma. He's disappointed.

When the trip is over and his feet come to rest again, his senses contradict what was running through his anticipating mindset. Immediately he tastes pungent, stale air. The comforting, ambient nature sounds, from before, run through his mind. *Where's the fresh mountain stream, a gentle wind, and birds singing, beautiful flowers and thousands of butterflies?* He can taste the air. The clean mountain air smell and the woody incense are gone. *Totally gone!* In their place are smells of car exhaust, old wood, and hot asphalt, and others better not identified.

Reluctantly, but finally Bob gets acclimated to his new environment, he's ready to find out where he is. It's hard to think with logic, reason and common sense all thrown to the wind. He slightly closes his eyes. *If I ask Malek what year this is, he's going to ramble around about the number one hundred again.* Halfway reluctantly, he enquires, "Where are we this time?"

Malek says, "We're in Lubbock, Texas in 1924.

After touring a small part of the city, Bob observes, "I can't believe the low prices of everything. A gallon of gas is eleven cents, a daily paper is a penny, men's Oxford shirts are a dollar, fifty-nine, milk is fifty-four cents a gallon, and record albums are three for a dollar.

Malek adds to what Bob's saying, "Yes, and the average home here costs $ 6,296."

They're having breakfast at an all-night dinner. It isn't a greasy spoon, but it is well on its way in that direction. "In the Jailhouse Now" is playing on the jukebox. Behind the café is a railroad, and across the street is an open field. The sky awoke in a good mood this Sunday morning. It's bright and a bit breezy. *Should be pretty all day.* Bob starts pontificating, "I remember a lot of things about this time, the Roaring Twenties. J. Edgar Hoover was appointed head of FBI. The ice cream cone rolling machine was invented. Johnny Weismuller set 100 mi. world freestyle swimming record at Miami. Diesel-electric locomotives came out. Babe Ruth, 'the Sultan of Swat,' was setting records. The Lone Ranger and Little Orphan Annie have just come out."

With a straight face, Malek enunciates his words precisely, "*Forsooth,* it sounds like you know all the main things." Then he rolls his eyes, which is his only indication of sarcasm.

Bob sniggers a little and replies, "Right, and I know the historical events. Remember, I teach history. It was a time of economic prosperity, rapid social change, and extreme optimism. The inflation rate was zero. The national wealth doubles between 1920 and 1929."

Suddenly, Bob changes the subject, asking, "What happened to Bruce and Molly?"

Malek remains silent for some time, then says, "They moved to Dallas, and he went into the furniture business."

The waitress changes the song on the jukebox to "Happy Days Are Here Again." Then she looks at them befuddled. It appears she wants to be a flapper, judging by her bobbed hair and loose knee-length dress. As she serves them coffee, she's thinking, *These two are a couple of bluenoses.*

Except for his chin jutting out, Malek shows no visual evidence of hearing what Bob has said. He is somewhat amused by the thoughts of the waitress. His posture is rigid and unmoving. His voice is flat, almost apathetic as he says, "*Bethink,* this time *tis* a period of cultural conflict. City-slickers are against small-town folks, Protestants are opposed to Catholics and perhaps worst of all, whites versus blacks. *Hence,* the new woman is against old-fashioned values."

Bob grins. "You're talking about flappers, right?"

The waitress refills their coffee cups and looks at them with a one sided head tilt and raised eyebrows.

As she walks away, Malek shares different info about the period of which Bob isn't aware. "U. S. population is 114,109,000. Average life span, in America, for men *tis* fifty-eight and for women sixty-five. The average American income *tis* less than $ 2,000 per year."

At that moment, a young man walks into the diner. He's thin and somewhat muscular. He has red hair, cut short. He also has a large upper lip and blue eyes. Immediately after entering the room, he says, "The usual," and sits at the counter.

In a subdued voice, Malek says, "*Behold,* that's Steve Randall, a high school drop-out, he *tis* your ancestor."

FIFTY-ONE: CAN THIS BE LUBBOCK?

Bob isn't impressed. What he says is, "Are you sure?" Immediately he leans forward. With some cynicism, he invades his personal space and passively listens. When Malek is slow to continue, he says, "He doesn't look too successful to me."

Malek responds, "*Aright*, he works for minimum wage, thirty-three cents an hour. Therefore, he stops by this diner for a cup of coffee *afore* meeting some friends. *Heretofore*, they play football across the street, in that vacant lot, every Sunday morning."

With coffee in hand, the young man leaves the dinner and walks briskly across the street.

Bob's a bit troubled. His saggy face is pale, and he's shaking his head. "He isn't in church today, on Sunday? That means he isn't a believer?"

Malek doesn't answer the question one way or the other. Instead, he points across the street. Two of Steve's friends have joined him. One of them, Buz Wilson, is heavy-set, with a small chin and large nose. He also has beady, brown eyes and a bulbous nose. The other, Richard Philips, has long shaggy brown hair. He's slim and gangly, wearing his pants hanging low. He has a dark complexion and brown eyes.

Malek announces, "*Verily*, I want you to listen to what those boys are saying."

With a dropped jaw, Bob says, "Omagosh," and it's followed by a quick bark of laughter. "You've got to be kidding. There's no way we can hear what those guys say this far away."

Before the three friends begin their conversation, Malek explains, "Steve *tis* a believer, but he has *nowise* gone to church in years." Then, he adds, "Steve's father was a drunk during these days of Prohibition, and then he left his family. His mother died three years later."

Bob's thinking, That sounds like my family.

Off-handedly, Malek remarks, "Would it not be interesting to hear what they are talking about?"

Bob's caught off guard. Why is he so persistent about this? What could these kids know about my ancestors?

"*Yea*, I will tell you what they are saying," Malek asserts.

Amazed, Bob asks, "For real, you can hear voices across the street?"

Malek answers, "*Forsooth,* I can hear voices across the state."

At this point, Malek begins to repeat every word said among the three friends, with appropriate accents.

"I ain't gonna beat yore gums. Did y'all 'ear 'bout the box job (train robbery) near Rondout, Illinois, last week?'

In his voice, which is like ice water, Malek explains, "The conversation is about the Newton Gang, a band of scurvy thieves who rob banks and trains."

He switches to Steve's voice again. "I'm telling you, they made a clean sneak. They're lousy wit money from the caper. They took in three million bucks, the biggest haul in history. The bulls don't have a clue. Wish we could do that well tonight at Benson Bank."

With that, he switches to the voice of Buzz Wilson, "Stop bumpin' our gums (that means talk about nothing.) You have all the equipment ready? Are you both heeled?"

Steve says, "I'm not packing, but I got a piece at home."

Wiping his runny nose on his sleeve, Buzz Wilson says, "I'll be packing heat tonight. You can't carry iron when you play football."

In Buzz Wilson's voice, he says, "My cousin, Brent Glascock, is a peterman, but he ain't gonna help us tonight."

Bob asks Malek, "What's a peterman anyhow?"

Malek explains, "It is a safecracker who uses nitroglycerin. *Yea,* the Newton Gang has robbed over seventy-five banks and robbed six trains in ten states and Canada. And they are sons of sharecroppers."

"Are you just beatin' your gums?" Steve enquires, and Malek repeats it.

"Buzz says, "I'm on the up and up."

Richard mouths, "I heard Joe and Jess, brothers of Willis, are living the high life, eating in the best restaurants, living in the lap of luxury, even driving a Studebaker.'"

Malek leans in to say, "Your ancestor says, 'I'm ready for some of that, myself.'"

FIFTY-TWO:
BANK ROBBERY IN THE MAKING

Malek's chin juts out, and his brow ruffles ever so slightly. Without any recognizable emotion, he says. "Come on, we need to get closer to this." The two of them cross the street and move to watch the young men. Now that they are closer, Bob softly says, "They do not have guns." Parked at the curb is a tin Lizzy. Malek and Bob take seats on the running board and try to get comfortable. Other young men begin arriving. They don't look much different from Steve and his two friends.

Before long, the game gets underway. Bob is asking himself, *What next?* Gus Philips is lean and gangly. Of the three, he's the most shabbily dressed. He's also the only one who has a bad case of acne.

The game gets underway. Bob and his two friends are on one side, and the four late-comers are on the other. Early on, Steve shows his prowess at football. Running, he's faster than a groundhog going down his hole. Passing, he's on the mark. On defense, he's formable. The game's fast-moving and physical in the extreme. Heads are smacked, feet are stomped, and tackles are made at every opportunity.

Bob turns around. There's another man standing beside them. *Who is this guy?* The man's short in stature, and his brown hair's streaked with gray. He has a bulbous nose and a full handlebar mustache.

The meaty man is almost recognizable. *There sure is something familiar about the man.*

The stranger introduces himself, "I'm Henry Dixon. I own this car." He waits a moment and then asks, "Who's winning?"

Malek jumps in with, "Our boy, Steve Bancroft, just threw a bomb."

Dixon, the stranger, replies, "Really?" he also starts watching the game. As the game progresses, Malek offers some play-by-play, "Look at that boy throw that ball. Talk about a gunslinger. Man, can he run."

They soon discover Dixon knows a lot about football. It isn't long before the stranger's talking up the game. "Did you see that bootleg?" In between, he's cracking his knuckles.

"Man, oh man, that's a first-rate pass to the coffin corner."

When the boys on the field take a break, the three spectators introduce themselves. That's when they find out the short little man, Henry Dixon, is a football recruiter for the University of Texas. His comment about Steve Bancroft is, "That boy's cornfed."

Bob asks him, "How did you come to be watching the game with us?"

Dixon declares, "Dad, gum it. My Tin Lizzy stopped on me." Saying that he points back to the Model T. All three of them have used it as a viewing platform. He frowns and asks, "Know a good mechanic? Oh, the boys are fixing to start again."

Malek and Bob meander back over near Mister Dixon's "Tin Lizzie." Bob's personally excited inspecting the car. He can't take his eyes off it, even though he has been sitting on it for an hour. His enthusiasm is undisguised as he remarks, "This's one more fantastic-looking Ford Model T." He walks around the car, riveting his eyes on each component and scrutinizes a few mechanisms.

Picking up on Bob's interest, Malek asks, "Did you know it sells for $290, this year, 1924? *So be it,* over fifteen million sold." Opening the hood over the engine, he explains, "It has a four-cylinder engine, with a top speed *nigh* forty-two mph. It also has a three-speed transmission. *Howbeit*, it is a two-speed and a reverse."

Bob is attentive and fascinated. His head is slowly nodding. "I didn't realize you knew anything about working on a Model T."

It doesn't show on his face. Malek's slightly impatient. What he says is, "I know enough to put this wire back on where I took it off."

FIFTY-THREE: DUMB DORAS

While Malek is working on the man's car, Dixon's talking football with Steve. At the same time, a new menace is approaching. Six young men, black, Caucasian, and Hispanic, are walking with a swagger coming down the sidewalk. They're playfully bumping into and lightly hitting each other as they stroll along. All are dressed extremely casually. As they shuffle along, Malek's perception sharpens, noting each gesture and motion. Getting closer, all six of them stop. All are wearing contempt faces, wrinkled noses, and sneering lips, with the corners of their mouth slightly raised. The leader of the group growls, "Out of the way, dumbass, dingleberries."

Another one of the group says, "Aguas (Watch out)!"

Unsure what to do, Bob looks at Malek. With cold, hard, calculating eyes and a voice like ice water, Malek says, "You skirts, got something on your minds?"

The flicker of irritation sparks in each one of the six. Mounting anger is also building up in each of them. Malek continues, "If you want to keep breathing, do not draw those bean shooters, any of you."

With mounting exasperation tightening in his throat, the boy in front says, "And what are you gonna do about it, Grandpa?"

Expressionless and inscrutable, his voice like a dark night, Malek says, "I'm trying to be a good Samaritan and save the lives of all you Dumb Doras."

The same kid breaks into deep-throated laughter, "Ha ha, teehee." The other five take up the rowdy Tee-hees. "You're going to save us? You need to close your head and hoof it outta here while you can."

FIFTY-FOUR: PROPITIOUS RETREAT

Confronted with six gang-members, Malek looks at Bob and then glances at the three boys who, during the half, have been sitting on the curb. With eyes that could cut through concrete, he says, "Those three behind me could beat the six of you like a tiger on a pregnant rat."

Bob's wondering, *Is that an ill-chosen metaphor?* The young man, wearing a flat hat and suspenders, understands it enough for flames of rage to leap through him. He doubles his fists and grits his teeth.

As though deliberately trying to enrage these young trouble-makers, Malek declares, "The six of you could not beat the two of us." With that, he points to Bob and himself. "Wait a minute," he now says, "The six of you couldn't even beat little old me all by myself."

The half dozen are throwing a fit. Malek then and there disappears. Everybody, Bob included, twists and turns, asking, "Where did he go?"

Before the mystery's resolved, Malek appears behind the same boy. Quickly and gently, Malek touches the boy's left ear. Faster than a chasing cheetah, the boy falls to the ground.

His friends are stunned. Gasps of surprise and raised eyebrows come from all five remaining faces. They are even more dumbfounded when Malek disappears again.

It doesn't take long before Malek's standing behind two more boys wearing flat caps, knicker pants, and Oxford shoes. Bob's smiling with a premonition of what's coming next.

As he suspected, Malek lays a soft hand on both of them. Their mouths open, but they're unable to speak. They, too, fall to the ground.

Bob smiles at the two guys remaining. They're gasping and expelling breath rapidly.

Fear rolls in over them like a massive dark storm cloud. After Malek releases them, they run back up the street.

Malek and Bob are alone again. Unexpectedly, on the spur of the moment, Bob asks, "Do you know anything about Huntington's disease?" Yes, it's the same question he asked before. Actually, it is a familiar path Bob has walked down several times. It haunts him tremendously.

Malek takes a fistful of steps, waits a couple of minutes, and then rolls his eyes before articulating the exact some words he spoke earlier, "Some of the symptoms of Huntington's Disease include tremors, slow or abnormal eye movements. Some of the other symptoms include depression, irritability, and suicidal thoughts."

In Bob's mind, he drags up thoughts with which he still isn't at peace. Somberly, he asks, "What about life expectancy?"

With genuine empathy in his tone, Malek answers, "When the illness is recognized at your age, life expectancy should be between twenty and thirty years."

Bob hears that and starts down a new contemplation road. *What does that mean to me?*

Does it make any real difference?

FIFTY-FIVE: OVERCOMING A DROPOUT

Henry Dixon is impressed, "That was one of the best sweeps I've ever seen, young man."

I hadn't planned on being here this morning," He's talking to Steve Bancroft. "I want to offer you a scholarship to play football at U.T...."

Steve's flabbergast. With raised eyebrows and an open mouth, he responds, "Really?"

He looks back and forth with a blank look on his face. His jaw goes slack, and he narrows his eyes. "You know I dropped out of high school, don't you?"

Suddenly, Dixon becomes stone-faced. Looking around, he says, "That could be a problem." He's collapsing in his chair, expressionless. Biting his mustache, he breaks eye contact with Steve. Swallowing hard, he shakes his head and says, "You'll have to pass an entrance exam."

Bob and Malek, at this moment, are entering the café for a cool drink. They have been wandering about exploring the city. They've seen the Lubbock County Courthouse, only eight years old. They plan on seeing the Migrant Labor Camps this afternoon. Just now, they're engaged in a discussion about Flappers. Bob expresses personal dislike for their bobbed hair and loose knee-length dresses. Malek mentions how they smoke and drink in public. Then, he adds, "And they keep saying unladylike things."

Neither of them notices Henry Dixon and Steve Bancroft are in the same restaurant, at a table across the room. Then and there, Steve cries, "Oh no!" That gets their attention, and Malek focuses on their conversation.

Imitating Steve's voice, Malek says, "There's no way. It's totally impossible for me to pass any entrance exam. I dropped out of high school In the tenth grade."

Bob looks at Malek, hoping for an explanation or an answer. For his part, Malek appears unsympathetic and completely unmoved. Changing the subject, he declares, "Do you know, the KKK *hath* two million members this year?"

Bob's immersed in thought. His brow is furrowed; his head tilts to the left. Malek ignores his speculative appearance. Instead, he moves their dialogue in a different direction. "Jazz music is really becoming popular these days. *Whithersoever*, older people object to 'vulgarity' and 'depravity' found in jazz."

Bob suddenly tunes in. "Jazz music? I like the improvisation and the swinging rhythm. But how can we help my ancestor?"

Pretending an ignorance he doesn't possess, Malek answers, "What can be done?"

FIFTY-SIX: TUTORING IN THE EXTREME

Bob's conflicted. It shows in his eyes as much as if they contained question marks. *Do I ignore what is none of my business? How would Steve respond to my intervention? If I butt in, will it make any difference?* He turns to Malek, hoping for some word of advice or even a hint of what he should do.

Malek's face is impassive, with no hint of any feeling. His eyes are blank, vacant. If Bob listens intently, it sounds like Malek is humming. "Hmmmmm." *What does that mean, anyway?*

Bob rolls his eyes. *What should I do?* For a moment, he listens to the music emanating from the jukebox. Jimmie Rodgers is crooning, "In the Jailhouse Now." He stands to his feet and takes a deep breath. Smiling broadly, he walks over to the table where Steve and Dixon are at an impasse. Nervously, he says, "I couldn't help hearing your conversation."

Dixon's response is unspoken agitation. He scrunches his face into a frown. Steve, for his part, his response is a forehead and nose wrinkled, and a questioning look. He doesn't say anything but irritation is on his face.

Sitting in a vacant seat, he asks, "Have you gentlemen considered using some accelerated tutoring? That way, you could pass the entrance exam."

Both of them are stunned. Blood drains from their faces. Steve gawks in disbelief.

Malek has now joined the confab, and he interjects, "You guys need to know that the very best tutor available is right here." With that, he points to Bob. "I personally know of a dozen men he got into college."

It's Bob's turn to be flabbergast. He's totally taken aback. Looking at Malek with an unspoken question, *What are you doing?* A chill freezes him in place so that he doesn't say a word.

Malek, with a forced and uncharacteristic enthusiasm, says, "With a week of intense effort, *thou* could ace that entrance exam."

Dixon stares at Bob as if waiting for an agreement or explanation.

Steve turns his head toward Bob, expecting a response as well. Bob feels like his head is spinning. *This isn't a matter of hours; it's a matter of days, and we might not make it even then.*

Malek declares, "*Mayhaps*, we could start this afternoon." To say Bob has a few misgivings would be an understatement.

For his part, Steve is hesitant, "I've been out of school two years now…"

Dixon offers, "You could give it a try. You know, nothing ventured, nothing gained."

After reigning in his emotions, Steve says, "Why don't we get together in the morning and discuss this?"

FIFTY-SEVEN: ON A STEAK OUT

Daylight has heaved its last sigh. Gone for the evening are the city's fetid smells, car exhausts, cigar and cigarette smoke, garbage, and hot asphalt. City noises are greatly reduced. As the night matures, these noises diminish even more. Bustling public traffic, screech and squeals of brakes, and wailing of sirens and a dozen other sounds are greatly diminished when the sun goes down. Tonight, there is no moon, and very few stars are visible. In other words, it's dark as night. Sordid air breezes through Bob's nostrils as he and Malek wait.

The two of them are on steak-out this dark Sunday night. They are out of sight, across the street from Benson National Bank. Bob is becoming a bit impatient, though they haven't been here very long. A car is approaching, causing Bob to become a little tense.

The car drives past them, rhythmically thumping. Bob relaxes and, just to pass the time, allows his mind to wander.

She's the love of my life. That beautiful oval face, like a morning in the springtime, smiles at me. She smiles with her lips, her eyes, and her heart. And that body, curved, elegant, and shapely, what a woman. The eyes of his mind scan her naked body from head to toe. *What he can't actually see, he imagines. Her bosom is jiggling poetry in motion. The way she laughs, the way she plays with her hair and how she whirls around. The way she looks at me and how it makes me feel. I can almost hear her softened voice, saying, "I love you."* A smile comes unbidden as he thinks about how she says, *"Chillax," instead of chill out."*

His reverie is suddenly interrupted. Another car is approaching. That car stops a few doors from the bank. The three men they've been expecting get out of the car. All three of them dutifully scan the area, just to be sure. Then, they head to the bank's back door, satchel in hand.

Their hesitation causes Bob to contemplate, *Wonder if they're thinking about changing their mind.* They're in the process of picking the lock on the back door of the bank when Malek, now standing behind them, says, "You boys need some help getting into the bank?".

Bob jumps in with, "It's a little late to do business with this bank, don't you think."

Steve and his two friends are startled. Steve gasps; Richard clenches his fists until the knuckles are white. Buzz's nostrils flare. He pulls a handgun out of his pants.

By means of electromagnetism, Malek causes all three of them to freeze in place. All three become completely immovable. Looking at the sky and turning first one way and then another, Malek says, "What we have here is an interesting situation." Each word is annunciated precisely, his voice is like ice water. He pauses a little longer than usual. Bob's certain his plan is to increase the fear of the three young men. Continuing, Malek says, "*Forsooth*, it was my intention to leave you three just like this until the police arrive." Once again, he pauses for effect. "*Howbeit*, Bob here wanted me to allow you boys to escape. *Methinks*, that *tis* not a good idea, as you will simply try to rob another bank, next week." After that, he rubs his chin, trying to suggest he's thinking.

Bob jumps into the performance, saying, "Maybe, just maybe, we could find a way to turn them loose with a commitment not to attempt another robbery?"

In a voice dark as night, Malek asserts, "I *nowise* believe these three would honor their word, if they gave it." With that, he takes the pistol out of Buzz's hand. Bob's surprised when Malek reaches around Richard and draws another gun from his waistband. He hands both guns to Bob. Next, he turns away from the three immovable characters. He doesn't say anything. However, he's actually aware of the growing panic among them.

After waiting for what must have seemed like an eternity for them, he turns back and faces them. His eyes are dark, like a shark's eyes that bore into their soul. "You know, *erlong,* you three are going to be arrested and will spend a prolonged period of time imprisoned. And all of you are intelligent. You could do great things have stellar careers." With that, he sighs. Bob sighs as well.

Malek releases them from their immobility. Richard is the first to say anything, "Whew!"

Then he says, "Finally," gleefully. He staggers back a step to lean on the bank's back door.

Buzz throws his hands in the air. "Hooray!" he says, with a glowing face. As he regains his composure, he starts rocking back and forth.

Malek slaps his thighs and says, "So be it." After a moment's pause, he adds, "You are free to go. You do not get the guns back, and that stolen car remains right where it is."

FIFTY-EIGHT: ATTITUDE ADJUSTMENT

The next morning, Bob and Malek are once again sitting in the same all-night café. Four other diners are already here. Louis Armstrong is singing, "Ain't Misbehaving," on the jukebox. Steve walks in, and the waitress smiles broadly. She brings him his coffee and leans in close to him. She asks, "Do you like this song?"

He shrugs. She lowers her voice and says, "My name's Daisy." He takes a sip of his coffee and half-heartedly smiles at her. Then he gets up and walks over to Malek and Bob's table.

After a moment's hesitation, he says, "Alright. I'm ready to go for it, but you will have to help me."

Bob's thinking, *I'm not sure how long it will take or how smart the kid is*. Still, he answers with, "Yeehaw." He feels a surge of satisfaction as he says, "We need to get busy, ASAP."

Malek doesn't appear to be excited. He offers a word of caution, "*Aye,* it will not be easy, and will require much concentration. If you aren't ready to work really, really hard, don't start, *nowise.*"

Tutoring gets underway. Instruction happens afternoons in a city park, mornings in a motel room, and late at night in the all-night café. Bob teaches him American history, dates, events, and personalities. He also instructs in world history, with a strong emphasis on Biblical history. Malek gives Steve a little intellectual boost by means of a casual touch on his head. Then he teaches him science and math. Toward the end of their sessions, he also gives him another uplift to his intellect. It takes time to cover all of the subjects, a lot of time. That means going from can, to can't, for eight days. Malek and Bob alternate, but Steve has to push through. Both tutors are impressed with his stamina.

There's also a great deal of stress and frustration. Steve declares, "I give up," no more than thirty times.

Bob says, "Come on; let's try it again," at least a hundred times. His patience is tested more times than ever before in his teaching career.

For his part, Malek repeats, "You need to concentrate," ad nauseam.

They also have to contend with detractions. The waitress, Daisy, keeps trying to take part in the process. When she's unable to participate, she tries to hear all that's said. And of course, she keeps changing the juke-box. "Ol' Man River," "Sweet Georgia Brown," and "Making Whoopee," are repeated over and over. Speaking of obstructions, there and then, a black man walks in and sits at the counter. He orders a burger and fries. He's lean and powerful looking. No formal clothing or Sunday-go-to-meeting clothes. He's dressed in work clothes.

Steve is in the middle of saying, "Ohio becomes a state…" He stops suddenly. Irritation crackles in him. Soon, he's seething. Malek can see it in his eyes and his raised eyebrows. Mounting exasperation tightens in his throat. Unable to resist any longer, he jumps to his feet.

Bob grabs his arm, asking, "Where you going?"

Steve snarls, "I'm going to get that black trash out of here." As he rushes to the counter, Bob is right behind him. Malek continues to sit observing.

In a belligerent and angry voice, Steve says, "Hey you!"

Two patrons at one table and two at another look around at the disturbance. Bob pushes between the two men. "What are you doing," Steve, demands Bob. It's obvious he's upset.

Clearly agitated, Steve answers, "I'm about to throw this dumbass out of here."

The black man doubles up both of his fists. Sternly but calmly, Bob says, "Listen to me. If you want my help, now or later, you will admit God made all men equal. You dare not treat some men as though they're animals." Then he turns to the black man and says, "Sir, please accept my apology for my friend's stupidity."

Days later, when all of the tutoring is finished, Steve takes a bus to Austin and the University of Texas. They are told it will take two or three weeks before they will know if he has passed or not.

FIFTY-NINE:
VISITING AN OLD FRIEND

Bob's deep in thought. His mind wanders across the wild waste of years. After a few minutes of silence between them, he says to Malek, "These last few days remind me of those years I was working my way through college. Went to school in the mornings and worked at a plywood plant at night. Work. Work."

Malek offers a retort, asking a question to which he already knows the answer, "What about your stepfather, Simon Crenshaw? Couldn't he afford to send you to college?"

Bob takes on a hang-dog expression because his heart has an open wound that won't heal. With his chin trembling slightly, He says, "My senior year in High School, dear old Dad took up with a woman half his age. He and my stepmother were divorced, and she passed away a year later." He waits for some comment, but none is offered.

He continues, "When I started college, Dad's new wife wasn't willing to spend that kind of money on me."

Malek comes up with a different thought, "Why do we not reduce these next three weeks of waiting down to a few minutes?" Bob's all to making this short-time jump. As they're getting ready, the thought ambles through Bob's mind, *How many weeks does this make I have been gone from home? All the days and nights amount to several weeks.*

The two of them do as they have done before. They reduce the three-week time, at least for them, down to a period of ten minutes. Still, Bob is fidgeting, cracking knuckles, and having trouble sitting still. For his part, Malek shows no impatience, in part because he knows the answer that's coming and in part because he enjoys watching Bob's nervous waiting.

The morning humidity is uncomfortably high. The air is thick and hot. The scene's the same, but the weather's different. Bob calms down when they get the word Steve was admitted to the University. Either from hearing what's on Bob's mind or from simple desire, Malek casually mentions, "No, we aren't going to jump ahead to watch Steve play football. We're running out of time together. I have other assignments."

Bob's surprised. His thinking goes into overdrive. *I never thought I would be dissatisfied with this adventure coming to an end. Will I ever see Malek again?*

"Does that mean we're going home," he asks.

Malek responds, "That's what it means."

Bob's thinking goes into overdrive. *Never thought I would be disappointed this adventure would end. Will I ever see Malek again?* He rubs his hand over his frizzy hair and looking at Malek, says, "I am proud of the difference we made in Steve's life."

Malek comes back with, "You are right. Steve will have a glorious football career at the University of Texas. After graduation, he will play professional football for a couple of years."

Bob can hardly contain his soul-stirring joy and pride. A cloud of excitement erupts over him. Then he stops and says, "You said for a couple of years. Does that mean he will be injured?"

"*Nowise*. He saves his money and goes back to school, medical school, and *betimes* he becomes a physician."

Excitement tingles through Bob. He's bouncing off the walls with hair-raising elation. "Do you think we might look in on him," he asks.

Malek looks at him with a penetrating stare. Bob isn't sure why he's looking at him or what's on his mind. *This whole thing's a great mystery. I never know what's going to happen next.* But he's delighted to hear Malek say, "I think I can arrange that."

At this point, he takes both of Bob's hands. The feeling of time travel has now become familiar to him. *After all that's happened, I still don't understand it.*

SIXTY:
A NEW DILEMMA

When they arrive at their destination, the unabashed clear blue sky welcomes them. They are on the sidewalk, in front of a home that might well be called trophy property. Bob is particularly impressed with the size of the house and the lush landscaping. His eyes blink rapidly as he tries to process all he sees.

A lady dressed in black and white answers the doorbell. Malek says, "We would like to see Dr. Steve Bancroft."

That lady smiles and says, "He isn't seeing anyone right now." She starts closing the door.

Malek stops her, saying, "Tell him the two guys who got him into college want to see him."

She closes the door, and they are left standing on the porch. As they wait, Bob scans the property, including their own tennis court and the two high-dollar autos in the drive.

Within a few minutes, the door opens again. A different lady greets them. She's giddy with obvious joy. Bob has no idea who she is. Without warning, she throws her arms around Bob and then Malek. She's giggling when she asks, "Don't you know me?"

Malek stands motionless. He offers no reply.

Bob takes a step back and makes a fake or tense smile. While averting his eyes, he says, "No, I don't think so."

Full of enthusiasm, she says, "I'm Daisy, Steve's wife."

"You used to be a waitress at that café in Lubbock," Bob says excitedly.

She bobs her head up and down as she acknowledges Bob is correct. Steve's going to be so glad to see you, especially right now." Then she starts walking away. "Come on, follow me," she says, back over her head.

Bob's impressed with the soaring ceilings and the lavish décor. Mentally, he's wondering, *What do they do with all of these rooms?* He's trying not to appear so agog as she ushers them into an oak-paneled den. Bob's not so much surprised by the room as he is by the three men inside it.

Seeing them, one of them jumps to his feet and hurries toward them. He grabs their hand and shakes them enthusiastically. "I am so glad to see both of you," he says. He looks at the two strangers in the room and says, "These men gave me the life I have. I am so grateful for these two who were there when I needed them." With that, he turns to the men standing near him. One of the two, the one with the bald head, shakes his head negatively. Bob's amazed at how different Steve looks. *I would never have recognized him.*

"I can tell something's wrong here," Bob declares.

At that, Daisy breaks out bawling. "Wa waah!" she runs to Steve and throws her arms around him. The anguish on Steve's face says his pain is a sharp knife in the gut. Malek stands erect with his legs apart and his fists on his hips. Bob's on the edge of fear, wondering, *What's going on here?*

At this point, one of the men pulls a badge, saying, "Dallas P.D., I'm going to have to ask you gentlemen to leave. This is a police matter, and we demand you two leave immediately."

His voice is loud and severe. His manner is deliberate and abrasive.

This is where Malek takes control. Calm as a summer day, he stares at both men, saying, "I am asking you to have a seat." Both men instantly become angry. The bald officer roars, "I don't know who you think you are, but you're about to be arrested for interfering with police." Obviously, having their authority challenged is unnerving to the officers.

Steve interjects, "Wait a minute. Let's hear what he has to say. I trust these fellows. Hear them out,".

One of the detectives, the one wearing the lop-sided glasses, looks at the other quizzically.

Steve pleads, "Hear them out."

Reluctantly, the two of them sit down again.

Malek explains, "You two are here because their daughter, Linsay, has been taken…"

Before he can continue, the slick-headed detective is back on his feet, yelling, "How do you know that?"

The other detective snarls, "You could be in trouble."

Bob speaks up, "He just knows stuff."

The other detective adjusts his glasses and aggressively snorts, "I'm going to have to take you down to headquarters." He reaches out a hand toward Malek. Then, he stops. He freezes in place. At this point, the other officer tries to figure out what's wrong with his partner.

Daisy looks at her husband, puzzled beyond words. Steve says, "Don't worry about them. I've seen this before. Malek's in charge."

Malek says, "All of us need to sit for a moment."

After the four of them are seated, Daisy points to the two officers, standing motionless. "What about them," she asks.

In what might pass for a cheerful voice, Malek says, "They're going to stand there until we get this worked out. Now, tell me this: have the kidnappers demanded money yet?"

Daisy says, "Yes, they have. I received a call this morning. They said we had to raise fifty thousand dollars. Said they would call back and tell us where to take it."

Malek walks over in front of the officers and says, "I know who these kidnappers are and where the little girl is. What we need to decide is what part you two are going to play." At this moment, he allows the two detectives to return to normal.

Dr. Steve Bancroft

SIXTY-ONE: BRING $5,000

Malek strides around the room. Then he stops, looks straight at Steve, and declares, "Richard Philips and Buzz Wilson are your kidnappers. You remember them, don't you, Steve?"

Before he can answer, Daisy says, "I do."

One of the officers stares at Steve and declares, "I don't know how this clown pulled this paralyzing trick, but I want to know how you know the men who have your daughter?"

Steve's agitated as he says, "Of course I know them; we were running buddies when we were teenagers, but I haven't seen either one in at least twenty years." The detective's eyes narrow, and he starts looking up and to the right.

That very minute, the telephone on the wall rings. Steve runs to answer it. "Hello. This is Steve Bancroft." He listens for a moment, then nods his head at Daisy. "I understand," he says, snapping his fingers. He points to a pad on the table. When Daisy gives it to him, he whips out a ballpoint from his pocket. He scribbles down an address on the pad. He's silent a moment and then says, "Yes, I understand."

The officer wearing glasses snatches the pad from him. Steve turns to Malek. "He said to bring $50,000 at exactly 2:30 this afternoon."

The detective with the large nose says, "We will stake out this trash bin and nab him when he grabs the money." With that, the two of them rush out.

Steve says, "I'll get the money from the bank and take it to the drop spot."

Malek cautions him, "Come straight back here; don't hang around. Let the cops pick up those two. Bob, you stay with Daisy and protect her. I will go get your daughter."

Daisy is beside herself. Her husband tries to comfort her with a hug before leaving. After everyone's gone, Bob tries to offer some encouragement. "What is your daughter's name," he asks.

She answers, "Her name is Emily."

To keep her mind off the activities taking place, Bob decides to tell her about his fiancé. "Her name is Belinda Wilson. Her eyes are denim blue, fringed with long lashes. Her hair is golden blond. Her legs are slender and curved. She has a coy smile and a face like a morning in the springtime. And she's poised and elegant when she moves."

He pauses a moment and then adds, "I better stop; just thinking about her turns me on."

Malek walks in the backdoor of an empty house on the south side of town. The vacant house looks as though it hasn't been lived in for a number of years. Two men are sitting at a table playing cards.

"Hello, boys," Malek says. They're startled and jump to their feet. All of the cards and the folding table go flying. "Do you remember me, Buzz," he asks of the now bald-headed man.

The other man, now wearing a beard wearing and glasses, angrily snarls, "I remember you. You're the dipstick who ruined our plans for our future years ago."

Malek says, "Men, we can do this the way we did all those years ago at Benson National Bank, or you can simply handover your weapons. Reluctantly, they hand him their handguns.

Then, they show him where the little girl is locked in another room. Her hands and feet are tied, and tape covers get mouth. He unties her and removes the tape. Lifting her up in his arms, he wraps his arms around her and hugs her warmly. Before releasing her, he tells Buzz and Richard, "If you two try to run, I will cut you down where you stand."

Coolly, Richard says, "I suppose you're going to let us go, like you did that other time?"

Malek has a stoic or blank facial expression. His eyes are dead, like those of a doll's eyes.

He says nothing else, and he stares at them with a cold, hard, calculating stare. Later, he softly tells Emily, "You will see Mommy real soon."

Buzz starts toward the door, saying, "Well, we'll see you around." Richard waves a farewell hand. They take three or four steps and then stop. Both of them are frozen in place.

Being immovable takes a few seconds to realize. Indeed, neither one can believe they are truly paralyzed, like before. Dark pools of fear appear under their eyes. Both men break out in sick, slimy human perspiration.

Hearing their thoughts as though they were spoken aloud, Malek knows they're wondering how long they will be paralyzed. He walks over to the door and begins waiting. He doesn't wait long before he can hear the police siren.

SIXTY-TWO: A NEVER ENDING SEARCH

Tears of joy flood Daisy's face when Malek walks in with Emily in his arms. The little girl reaches out her arms, saying, "Momma." Happiness resounds through her mother; she has never felt so alive before. She hugs her daughter like she never intends to let go. "Oh, thank you, Malek," she says with tears in her eyes.

Bob introduces himself to the little girl, "My name is Bob; I helped your Dad get into college a long time ago." A few moments later, Steve hurries into the room, and the real celebration gets underway.

A couple of hours later, Bob and Malek are out on the street once again, looking for a spot where they can inconspicuously take their trip back to Bob's present. As they walk, Bob confides in Malek, "You know, I'm really glad we were able to help Steve again." To himself, he says, *It makes me feel good helping people.*

The defender agrees and adds, "*For sooth*, Steve will have a long and productive career. During his career, hundreds of *divers* people will be helped. Indirectly, *wherefore* you will be a part of helping each one."

Since Bob is so overjoyed, Malek discloses, "*Erelong*, Steve will have a son along with this daughter. That son, Bryan, will be a not-so-quiet individual. When he has *nought* to say, he still says it. He thinks everyone deserves his opinion. This daughter, Emily, will become a *sore* good person. She marries a man named Brad. *Forsooth,* he will be indolent. Few men have come close to being as lazy as him. But he will always find a reason for not doing what he should, 'I'm waiting for the right time, I don't feel good,' or, 'I have too much stuff to do.' And he likes to make up stories. He *verily* will tell people about the battles he supposedly fought. He will boast about being close friends with the governor. That *scurvy* fellow will even tell people how he went to sea and *thenceforth* worked his way up to captain." Malek shakes his head.

Suddenly, he changes the subject. "*Thou* feels pride for making such a difference in someone's life." He pauses a moment, then adds, "Thou should realize you do this same thing for the hundreds of other students you have taught and will teach."

Bob sighs and comments, "Yes, it's a great life." Off the cuff, Bob says, "Can you tell what I'm thinking?"

Without any physical response, he answers, "Of course."

Bob replies, "I knew it. I knew it." Clearly, he's pleased with himself. "I figured out you know what's going on in my head." Still, he isn't ready for what comes next.

"When we get to know each other a little better, we'll communicate back and forth without saying a word."

"Astounding," Bob says, with a skip in his step. "Another thing I wanted to ask, would it be possible for me to see my birth mother?" Malek says nothing in response.

Without affecting the flow of time, Malek uses tempokinesis to change their position, both in place and time. In a split second, they move night to daylight. They also move from Steven's neighborhood to another sidewalk, outside another restaurant, in a different city.

Here, the sky is clear and completely cloudless, and the air is almost tropical. The area itself has something of a familiarity to Bob. The name of the restaurant is "Gilbert's, a name well-known to Bob. The thought runs through his mind. *I think I've been to this place, maybe with Belinda.*

Inside, the place is well-decorated, and the atmosphere is welcoming. They're met by a hostess who shows them to a seat. Bob takes a deep breath, trying to identify the aroma in the air. The smoky smell of meat roasting and the buttered aroma of fresh bread makes his mouth water. Other aromas mix and mingle with those.

Bob leans forward and facetiously says, "You know, I'm glad we're eating at a little better place than you usually take us to."

As the waitress approaches, Malek nods his head. Bob isn't sure if he simply wants to call his attention to her or *Is he identifying my mother? Does he already see something else?* The waitress is appropriately polite. She's extremely thin, with dark hair. She has deep-set, nut-brown eyes, which make her brow appear more pronounced. There is something disquieting about her, though Bob can't identify what it is. Her voice is somewhat throaty, bordering on quavering. "What will you have, gentleman," she asks, with a forced smile.

They order a meal consisting of mixed vegetables and meatloaf. As is usual with Bob, they go for the cheapest thing on the menu. It is at this point Bob's concluding, *This woman cannot be my mother, and she can't be found here*. When the waitress has written down their order, Malek says, "I would like to see the manager, please." Of course, Bob's wondering, *What's going on? What has he got to complain about?*

When the manager arrives, she is a well-dressed black woman. She's extremely thin, with kinky, black hair, already turning gray. It is piled artistically on top of her head. She has dark, smoldering eyes with sparkle in them. She also has exceedingly long eyelashes.

Even though middle-aged and better, Bob thinks, *She's knock-you-off-your-feet beguiling.*

Mrs. Jamila Wilson

Appropriately polite and in a softened voice or tone, she says, "Gentlemen, I'm Jamila Wilson, General Manager here. What can I do for you?"

There is a sophistication, if not genuine pride, about the woman. She stands erect with her chin high and a broad smile enveloping her face. That is, until Malek says, "I would like to introduce to you your son, Bob Becker."

The smile instantly vanishes from her face and she looks as though she has been hit in the face. When she's able to gather her composure, she mumbles, "Whatever do you mean?"

She may be confused, but Bob's stunned. This can't be right. How could this black woman be my birth mother?

SIXTY-THREE: IS THIS MOTHER?

In a kind, gentle tone, Malek says, ""On June thirteenth, 1998, at Baptist Hospital, in this city, you gave birth to a son." Hearing that, she sits down and bows her head. Malek continues, "Like seven million other Americans, the son to whom you gave birth is of mixed blood, a Halfrican, if you will."

Bob is incredulous. *How can this be? No way*. He looks to Malek for an answer, but none is forthcoming. He's totally at a loss. His eyebrows are drawn together in a tight downward arch. His jaw goes slack.

Jamila raises her head. She's bawling her head off. Tears are streaming down her face. In between the squalling, she's desperately sucking in breaths. She sobs, "Are you sure?"

Malek places a hand on her hand saying, "Yes, I am sure."

Bob is engulfed in a thundercloud. Is this woman really my mother? Can this be the lady who brought me into the world? If she is, how should I feel? Should I love her or resent her? His thoughts have his mind in knots.

Jamila is still blubbering and moaning. Neither Malek nor Bob says anything. Instead, they sit and watch her weep for a while. Finally, she manages to control her sobbing. "Sniff, sniff." And at last, she says, "You have to understand, I never wanted to give you up for adoption. My husband. . ."

At this point, Malek jumps in saying, "Bob, you remember our preacher friend in St. Louis, Jerry Bancroft, do you not?"

Bob nods his head. However, a questioning thought intrudes into his consciousness.

What could he possibly have to do with my birth?

Malek continues, "If you recall, the preacher had a son they named Jeremiah. He, in turn had a son, he called Larry. The father and son were both religious men. Larry had three sons. The middle son, Felix, liked people. That is, if they were like him; if they weren't, he hated them." Jamila is nodding her head and wiping tears from her face. Malek looks at her, as he says, "He took part in the infamous Tulsa Race Riot."

Looking at Malek, Bob frowns with an expression that says, "I don't know what you mean."

Malek explains, "It was a rolling gun battle that began on Memorial Day, 1921. A mob of white people looted homes and stores belonging to black people. Ten thousand people were left homeless, and over three hundred people were killed. Felix Bancroft fully participated in that horrible event. He was also an active member of the Klu Klux Klan. He took part in several lynchings of black men. I can give you names and dates if you like."

Jamila has gotten control of her emotions, and she says, "He had a son, he named Ezra.

He abused him horribly, beating him regularly. Growing up, Ezra came to hate his father."

She pauses a moment and places her hand on Bob's. She continues, "At seventeen, he ran away from home. Looking back on it, I think he married me, at least in part, out of spite for his Dad." She stops and looks deep into Bob's eyes. "I can see a lot of him in you, especially those blue eyes." But she's trembling or shivering as she listens intently. She has a beaming expression with a genuine smile. It takes almost no time for her to feel deeply connected to this young man. Everything in her world feels exciting and new to her. As she has always, before today, she wants nothing but the very best for him. She can't help remembering all the nights she wondered where he was and what he was doing. Through her sprints recollections of the hundreds of times, she has prayed that he would be doing well. So many, many times she longed to see him. Not a day went by when she wasn't hungry for an opportunity to talk to him.

Malek breaks into her memories, saying, "Tell him what happened."

She explains, "When I was expecting you, a relative of Ezra, a cousin or something, found us. He said Felix was looking for us. Said he would kill us both and our baby. It was horrible. I was having hot and cold flashes and headaches that were excruciating. Because of his fear of impending doom, Ezra had difficulty breathing. And he was terribly irritable."

She is now staring at Bob with an empathetic and loving look. She has a beaming expression while leaning toward them.

Malek says, "Allow me to tell the rest of the story. Jamila and Ezra agreed they could never be safe together. Ezra knew all too well his father would never shrink from murder.

So, as hard as it was, reluctantly, they decided to separate and give the baby up for adoption to keep him from Felix." Bob's nodding during Malek's revelation, with a dour appearance.

Softly, she whispers, "I never stopped loving you. There has never been a single day since your birth when I didn't think about you. I would try to imagine what foods and what colors you might like." She has to stop for a moment. Her eyes are filled with tears, and she's choking. As she begins again, her voice has a lilt that makes you think of butterflies and tinkling bells. "I kept seeking answers, from the hospital, from Human Services. Nobody would tell me anything. On your twenty-first birthday, Tyrel and I celebrated, even though he has never seen you. We joined hands, and both prayed you would be alright and that you would do well."

Tears of joy are now streaming down Bob's face, kind of a real flower garden face.

Suddenly, Jamila stands to her feet and says to Bob, "Stand up." Slowly and a bit nervously, Bob stands to his feet.

When he does, Jamila throws her arms around him and hugs him fervently. When she releases him, she says, "I want to take you to my house so you can meet the rest of your family.

Malek answers, "You certainly can, but is it alright if we finish our meal first?"

SIXTY-FOUR: METHAMPHETAMINE OR CRANK

Bob and Malek are in Jamila's car as she drives them to her home. The SUV still has that "new car smell," which impresses Bob. After they have ridden a ways, Bob remembers this part of the city. It isn't the most luxurious section of the city, but it certainly houses those who are doing well. Bob is enjoying the scenery when he hears Jamila say on her cellphone, "Tyrell, I need you at home as soon as you can get there. Yes, and I love you too."

The house is more than Bob expected, not lavish but substantial. The lawn is beautifully landscaped and well-kept. They enter the house through a side door leading them into the den. The oak-paneled den has a cathedral ceiling with a balcony. The furnishings and the décor are all top-notch. Bob is appropriately impressed, while Malek is unaffected. He doesn't yawn, but his facial expression has no delight in it. As they take seats, Jamila yells, "Reginald, Javon, come here!"

In a matter of minutes, two teenage boys come tromping down the stairs from the balcony. Curiosity is written all over both their faces. The young men have raised eyebrows and a slight smile.

Without prologue or explanation, Jamila says, "Boys, I want you to meet your brother, Bob Becker."

Both emit small yelps. With a shaky voice, Javon says, "But he's a white man."

Reginald puts his fingers against his mouth.

At this moment, a tall black man enters from the same door the others came through. He quickly surveys the room and asks, "What's up, guys?"

Jamila walks over to him and says, "I want you to meet Malek. I don't know his last name, and Bob Becker." Tyrell shakes both of their hands warmly.

Then he says, "To what do we owe the honor of this visit?"

With a face surrendered to bliss, Jamila says, "Bob is the son I gave up for adoption."

Bob's sitting still, with some effort, wonders, *Is he going to get mad? Will he insist we leave immediately?* He studies the man's face meticulously but can't discern how he's taking this revelation.

All he sees is eyebrows high and curved and a lowered jaw. Suddenly, his expression changes. His eyes become big and bright. In a softer voice, he says, "I am delighted to meet you, Bob. Your mother told me all about you several times through the years. I'll have to tell you, both of us have for years wished we could actually meet."

During the better part of the afternoon, they all share with each other. That is, Bob and his new family share where they have been, what they have done and not done as well as what they've experienced. It's a warm and informative conclave. Jamila tells them about how she went back to school and struggled to get an education; she told them about meeting Tyrell.

Bob tells them about his two foster families, about his working through college on his own, and about how much he enjoys teaching and helping young people. Tyrell explains he enjoys business and, especially, owning and operating his own business.

With something of a sneer in his voice, Reginald says, "Bob, let me ask you something."

Bob's answer is, "Sure."

Reginald continues, with a bit of a snigger, "Being a mixed breed, do you still feel like you're superior to us blacks?"

"Reggie," his mother says. "That's no way to talk to your brother."

Bob calmly says, "Reginald, I believe all men are the same in the eyes of God, and I hold that to be true. I teach white students, black students, Hispanic and Oriental students. I treat them all the same, and I care about each one."

A subtle flash of pride slips across Jamila's face. Her husband looks at her and smiles reciprocally.

Then and there, Malek says, "Reginald, may I ask you a question?" His response is a one-shoulder shrug.

Standing to his feet, Malek looks straight into his eyes. He then asks, "Do your mother and father know you are taking Methamphetamine, or as you call it, Crank?"

His mother is shocked as she says, "No, tell me that isn't so." Anger is beginning to build in his father's face. Mounting exasperation tightens in the throat, and his eyebrows lower. His breath quickens, and he crosses his arms over his chest. The corners of the mouth point downward.

Reginald starts for the door. Back over his shoulder, he says, "I don't have to listen to this."

Malek employs ionized particles or molecules to interact with electric fluids to provide a ray from his eyes to Reginald. The boy is frozen in place. His eyes fly open wide. Astonishment goes from his head to his gut.

Malek then walks over to where he's standing in front of the boy. His legs are spread, his shoulders are back, and his chin is high. Both fists are on his hips. He stares intently at the immobilized teenager as he asks, "Do your parents know you and a buddy burglarized a neighbor three doors down from here two nights ago?"

Tyrel is stunned and growing in rage. He demands, "How do you know this?"

Malek softly says, "Calm yourself, Sir. Your son's share of the loot they stole is even now upstairs in Reginald's bedroom closet." With that, Malek goes quiet.

The father nods to Javon, and he runs hurriedly upstairs. Jamila is anxious and starts wringing her hands. A few minutes later, he walks back down, carrying a bag full of loot.

Tyrel examines the contents and allows his wife to inspect them as well. A swell of rage rises on Tyrel's face. Disappointment floods Jamila's veins.

Malek scans Reginald once again. He can easily see the fear in his eyes, no doubt from suddenly being unable to move in any way. There are tiny movements around his eyes, however. He is unable, of course, to move his partially open mouth. Still, spittle is slobbering down his chin, and goosebumps cover each arm.

Malek says, "*Howbeit*, normally it would be of no concern to me that you have chosen to destroy your life. After all, it is your choice. But you are brother to my friend Bob, whom I care about greatly. I see fear in your eyes. I hear fear in your mind, and you should be afraid.

If you are so *beef-witted* as to continue down the track you have chosen for *thine* own, *forsooth* you will be dead within twelve years." Looking at his parents, he says, "I can tell you the exact month, day, and hour if you wish."

Malek releases the young man from his paralysis. He turns both of his hands over, staring at them. Then he raises his arms slightly. Tears are now streaming down his eyes as he runs to his parents. They hold him closely. Then Tyrel says, "Malek, we will straighten him out. You can count on that."

Bob says, "I'll be glad to help in any way I can. I live only a few miles away from here. Javon, I'll be glad to help you with your football skills."

SIXTY-FIVE: BACK TO BELINDA

Bob and Malek take their last time-leap journey. It's a short trip, three minutes and a few miles. After completing this trip in a matter of seconds, Malek comes out with, "*Certes,* my friends, this is where we part." With that, he wraps his arms around him and hugs him close.

Bob's getting emotional as he says, "I'm going to miss you, my friend." He really has to work at keeping the tears back.

Malek responds, "I will *nowise* be far away if you ever need me. When the Father calls you home, I will come and get you."

After the two of them say their goodbyes, Bob's lost in thought. *I now have a family with an invitation to visit anytime. I also have two brothers who are going to need my help from time to time. I have a new appreciation for my teaching profession.* When his feet hit the ground in the park, a feeling of delight sweeps over him. *It's good to be home.* Absent-mindedly, Bob cracks his knuckles as he walks back to where he left his car. *I hope it's still here after all of this time.* Out of habit, he raises his right arm and checks the time on his watch, 5:30, "Hmm." At this point, it hits him. *Where has my watch been for all these weeks? I have been away. I never saw it once. And why did I never miss it?* He gets in his car and drives straight to Belinda's house. *Feels so good driving down familiar streets.* He smiles as he passes the school where he teaches and the church where he worships.

After driving into her driveway, he feels a sense of unease and even trembles a bit.

When she opens the door, he is struck by her beauty. Her kissable red lips. *Look at her coy smile.* Her breasts are jutting like two young mountains. He hurriedly wraps her in his arms.

He kisses her passionately. The kiss is prolonged and sensuous. Holding her moves him in several ways.

When he releases her, she says, "I've been worried about you; you're over an hour late. I've been anxious to hear what the doctor said this afternoon."

Bob's blown away. This afternoon? I've been gone three and a half weeks. How can this be the same day? A barrage of questions storms instantly into his mind. *Where do I start? How do I explain to her and get her to understand what happened to me when I don't understand it myself? How do I explain my having a black mother and two black brothers? How do I make her understand how devastated I was learning I have Huntington's Disease? Should I tell her I found out I will live another thirty to fifty years? How do I explain I relish the idea of being her husband for any amount of time?*

He struggles to put all other thoughts out of his mind so he can share with her all he has experienced. Even so, another frightening question raises its head. *How will Belinda feel about being married to a man of mixed race?*

He suggests she sit down as he tells her a narrative hard to believe. He starts with his appointment with the doctor and his emotional reaction to it. He tells her about the individual he first thought was a man and turned out to be something else entirely. "He's a celestial agent assigned to help me." At this point, he stops and catalogs the various abilities Malek has. First, he tries to explain quantum mechanics, space-time, and time dilation. "Time is not 'passing' or 'flowing.' It just is. Time travel, or time-shifting, is achieved through the use of the time-dilation effect of what men of learning call Special Relativity. That's what Malek explained to me."

Next, he describes what Malek looks like and then adds, "Don't let that give you the notion he's just like us. That's the mistake I made. He always appears guarded, as if he were cold and hard. His eyes change color, from penetrating blue to black as a shark's eyes. When he talks, he enunciates his words precisely. Some of his words, like *afore* and *asunder* are archaic. He never cries or shows any emotion. He has the ability to understand 374 different languages. He can harness the power of his mind to control others. He has superhuman intelligence that far surpasses that of the most gifted and brightest humans. And he can manipulate time, to accelerate or slow it down. He can see she is at a loss for words. Her eyes narrow, and she starts chewing on her lower lip. Bob seeks to reassure her, "I know it's hard to come to grips with. I struggled with how it could be each and every time we traveled through time."

Bob starts a condensed version of what he has gone through. "The first trip we made was to Alexandria, Virginia, at least what would become Alexandria. There, we met a young man named Ryan Logan. We helped him escape, and six years later, we, well, more Malek than me, defeated a renegade band of Indians who intended to kill them. His wife Teata, a Cherokee Indian, was precious, and you can't imagine how cute their little son was."

She is listening to him empathetically.

"Then we made a hundred-year leap and landed in a brush arbor revival. There, we met the nicest family, the Mitchells. Their son Leroy was thrown into jail for something he didn't do. We helped him escape, and six years later, we went to see how he was doing. He now lived in St. Louis and had changed his name to Lewis Bancroft. He and his wife, Neomi, had gone into the ministry and were helping slaves escape to Illinois."

Clearly, she's wonderstruck. She's wearing a slight smile and breathing slowly. He tries to decipher what she's thinking from the expression on her face.

Deciding she's following him, he says, "Another thing Malek taught me is 'Reality is the totality of all things.'" He then tells her about Steve Bancroft and how they recovered their kidnapped little daughter.

He hesitates a moment and then continues, "When we came back to this city, I met my birth mother. Turns out she's a black lady." He waits to see the shock on her face, if it's there. It doesn't come. He studies her carefully. His cheeks are flushed, and his mouth's ajar. He's as mixed up as lentil soup.

Belinda picks up on his bewilderment. Her eyes twinkle, and she giggles. Then she says, "Come here." She hugs him and says, "I'm so happy you're in my life. I love you, and I've known all along that you're biracial. I will always love you."

Joy streaks through him like a comet. His heart's singing. He never felt more alive. *I worried for no reason.* He hugs her again as tears of joy stream down his face.

Later, in a quiet moment, total realization comes over him. With Malek, I have achieved a great deal. In the days ahead, I will accomplish other things that matter. I am somebody.

The End

MEET THE AUTHOR

The writer of this book grew up on the poor side of town in Memphis, Tennessee. He was the oldest of six children. At an early age, he would spend endless hours creating stories in his mind. He also spent a great deal of time drawing pictures.

At the age of fourteen, he felt a definite calling to enter the ministry. When he discussed this possibility with his father, his dad told him, "You better give up that idea. No way will you ever get the education required for such a profession."

Two years later, he met a young lady, later he would marry, and with whom he would spend the rest of his life. With her help and a lot of work, he earned three different degrees. With her by his side, he entered a pastoral ministry that would last sixty-four years.

Now, in the twilight of life, he's still making up stories. He's also drawing pictures to go with them.

Made in the USA
Coppell, TX
25 July 2025